McBride Rides Out

It all began when the Buckthorn Kid smashed his way out of jail. Before long there was a $40,000 hold-up on the railroad, and then murder and mayhem in Medora . . . Montana rancher Randolph McBride is on the trail of stolen cattle when he discovers the rustlers have joined forces with the train robbers . . . Now the lead really begins to fly and McBride's life is on the line. Will his fight for justice succeed?

JOHN DYSON

McBRIDE RIDES OUT

Complete and Unabridged

LINFORD
Leicester

First published in Great Britain in 2005 1

Gloucestershire County
Council Library

British Library CIP Data

Dyson, John, *1937 –*
    McBride rides out.—Large print ed.—
Linford western library
1. Western stories
2. Large type books
I. Title
823.9'14 [F]

ISBN 1–84617–393–0

Published by
F. A. Thorpe (Publishing)
Anstey, Leicestershire

Set by Words & Graphics Ltd.
Anstey, Leicestershire
Printed and bound in Great Britain by
T. J. International Ltd., Padstow, Cornwall

This book is printed on acid-free paper

1

'Hell!' a man shouted as an explosion billowed out flame and smoke and a great hole was blasted in the wall of the guard house at Fort Laramie, Wyoming. When the cloud of falling, splintered timbers and iron bars cleared, a young man in striped prison issue peered through the rubble into the dark wet night.

The Buckthorn Kid's face, blackened by the explosion, split into a grin. 'Think I used a tad too much dynamite. Must be losing my touch. Come on, boys!'

He leapt through the hole and raced across the wide parade ground followed by a dozen other convicts. Lanterns were lit in the barrack-rooms and there were cries from soldiers and guards as the prisoners went slipping and sliding in the mud. Suddenly, a Gatling gun on a guard turret started rattat-tatting, its bullets tracing a deadly pattern across the parade ground. One of the convicts screamed as he was hit in the foot and went hopping about as the others scattered in an attempt to escape.

Buckthorn lost his footing and dived face-first into a pool of horse dung. 'Shee-it!' he gasped aptly, staying low, waiting for the machine-gunner to chase his bullets after his cell mates. 'Now!' he hissed, and ran as fast as the mud allowed for the stockade wall directly below the turret. He pressed his back against the wall of solid adobe as the sheeting rain runnelled through his cropped hair. He was out of range of the gunner above him, but now troopers ran like disturbed bees from their beds and were firing carbines and revolvers at the striped-garbed escap-ees, who were dashing hither and thither like panicked sheep every whichaway.

'That's right,' the Kid muttered, licking the rain from his lips, and looking wildly along the wall for any sign of his accomplice. 'Keep 'em busy, boys.' That's why he had invited them along, as decoy ducks to be potted at. 'Where'n hell's she gotten to?'

He began to curse, thinking the breakout had been all in vain, when suddenly he saw a rope with a pronged grappling iron on its end snake over the wall. He ran to get a hold of it, gave the grappling iron a whirl and hurled it up to catch on top of the wall. He gave it a tug, and started to haul himself up, his boots scrambling to make purchase with the baked clay of the six-foot thick wall of the fort. More flares were being lit and the snarl of a rifle bullet smashing into the wall too close for comfort informed him that he had been spotted.

'There he is!' a soldier shouted. 'Stop him.'

The kid grabbed at the top of the wall, his muscular shoulders hauling him up to sit astraddle. Lead began whining and ricocheting off the adobe as he pulled up the rope and fixed the grappling iron into another crevice. 'So long, suckers!' he yelled. But the cocky grin was wiped from his face as the Gatling-gunner found him and a burst of bullets nearly cut him off at the knees.

'Yee-ow!' He gave a yelp of alarm, swung over the wall with the alacrity of a polecat, and slid down the rope to terra firma. 'The bastards,' he gasped out. 'They were trying to kill me.'

'Howdy, Kid. What took you so long?' What appeared to be a slim young cowpoke, in a floppy-brimmed hat and rain-shiny rubber slicker, welcomed him. 'I was about to give up on you.'

'God dammit, Della, I said midnight and I meant midnight.' The Kid was trying to climb onto a feisty mustang she had along. 'What's the matter with this bronc? You get him from a rodeo?'

'You musta spooked him, Kid. He don't like the look of you. You do look purty weird. Wouldn't care for you

4

gittin' on me, myself, if I was a bronc.'

'Hold still,' Buckthorn shouted, as he struggled to get a foot in a stirrup and swing onto the slippery saddle. 'You lousy piece of crowbait, what you buckin' for?'

'We better hurry it up, Kid,' Della drawled. 'Looks like they're opening up the main gate.'

'Right, let's ride.' He gave a shrill Indian yell, half-Sioux that he was, himself, and sent the mustang haring away down the slope towards Laramie stream, splashing through it and hauling the horse around to head up-river following its course. 'We'll lose 'em in the hills.'

The girl went charging after him as a bugler back at the fort began to blow 'boots and saddles'. But by the time a line of troopers filed out of the gates the two outlaws were well away swallowed by the darkness of the night and the drenching rain.

'So where we headin' to?' the girl asked, as dawn lightened the grey sky some hours later and they paused to give their horses a rest. It was a steep climb up through the granite cliffs of the pine-swathed Black Hills. 'What's all the hurry? You only had another six months of your sentence to do.'

'Something's on,' the Kid muttered, darkly, as he stripped the sodden cotton prison jacket from his lean, but muscle-honed body. 'It's on the grape-vine. Something big. I ain't missing out.' He tore away the soggy bottoms of the prison suit and tipped a pair of patched jeans and blue wool shirt from the canvas bag she had brought. 'What's this? You trying to make me look like some hick?' He pulled out a battered hat and tried it on. 'What's this crap? I told you to bring me some gear.'

'It's all I could get. I'm short of cash.' Della giggled, as she watched the kid struggle into a too-tight tweed jacket, his wrists protruding from the arm-holes. 'You look a real dude.'

'What are *these*?' he moaned, looking at the worn brogans. 'Couldn't you get some boots? I got my reputation to think of. I've allus been renowned as a snappy dresser.'

'Not today, you ain't. Be thankful for small mercies. I got you out, didn't I?'

'What about a piece?' He groped around in the bag and produced an ancient revolver. He raised it to one ear, listening as he cocked the hammer and the cylinder turned. 'It's as rusty as a farm gate. What the hell use is this?'

'There's some slugs in your coat pocket, mister. Heck, Buckthorn, I got it from a pawn shop in Cheyenne. Beggars cain't be choosers, you know. That bag of dynamite cost me a fortune. I might have blowed myself to Kingdom Come, carrying it in there under my knickers and that's all the thanks I git.'

The Kid sighed and stuffed the revolver in his pocket, looking back down the slope of trees and boulders for twenty miles through the mist towards Laramie Creek. 'Cain't see no sign of 'em. I figure we can take a short break. It ain't wise to light a fire, but, hell, I'm dying for a cup of cawfee. I presume you've brought some of *that* along?'

'Sure.' Della pulled a dented coffee pot from her saddle-bag and a small sack of coffee beans. 'You go find some kindling. I got some bacon, too. We might as well have a fry-up. I'm starvin'.'

'Yeah, me, too.' He left her to pound at the beans with her revolver butt, while he sought under the pines for some dry wood. When they had got a small fire started he loose-cinched the mustangs and gave them a handful of split-corn each. He pulled a roll of tarpaulin-covered blanket from behind his saddle and lay out on it beneath an overhang of rock. He watched the flames lick around Della's frying pan, heard the bacon sizzle and his belly groan. 'That sure smell's good.'

Della looked over and smiled at him warmly. 'Breakfast will be served in a few seconds, sir. Pity we ain't got no eggs. At least it's stopped raining for a bit.'

'Yeah, it's nice to feel dry.'

The food was good. Anything was good after prison food. The Kid had served four and a half years of a five-year sentence but he had never taken to the regime. It was good to smell the resin from the pine knots hissing as they burned, to be out under the great big cloudy Wyoming skies again. To be free. He felt like a new man.

'So, where did you say we were going?'

'I didn't. But, if you really want to come along it's due north to Deadwood to see my pal. That'll give him a surprise.'

'Are you sure that's wise? We ran into trouble there once before, don't you remember? Nearly got ourselves hanged.'

'Aw, why worry, Della? Anyway, I gotta git me some new duds. No self-respectin' cowboy can go around lookin' like this. We won't stay long. I tell ya, there's something big going on. They'll be needing an explosives expert like me.'

Della gave a guffaw. 'The Dynamite Kid. That's what they oughta call you. Remember how you blew up a whole damn boxcar, the safe, the cash and all? Ten thousand dollars fluttered away on the breeze.'

'We all make mistakes. It's part of the learnin' process. You know, Della, I been cooped up a long time without a woman.' A smile flashed across his handsome face as he lay back on the soogans and pulled her towards him. 'Even you look pretty good right now.'

'Even me?' She struggled to push him off. 'Why should I? You always were rotten to me.' But, even so, she tossed away her man's hat and stroked a hand through her cropped hair, studying him, her thin, full-toothed face, serious. 'I've never once heard you say you love me. Nor even thank me for visiting you and gittin' you out.'

'Thank you? Sure, I'll thank you. I'll

buy ya a new dress. But love? What's love got to do with it?' He caught her by the scruff of her neck and pulled her down towards him. 'Git on with it, gal. You do what you're best cut out to do an' we'll get along fine.'

Della arched her neck, tensing against him, then relaxed, giving him a smile. 'You know you really do love me, Kid, underneath, don't you? We're two of a kind. Come on, give me a kiss first, at least.'

'Women,' he groaned, pulling her face to his. 'You know I don't go for this kissin' stuff. It must be the Injin in me.'

* * *

One hundred and forty miles due north from Fort Laramie as the crow flies — if a crow should fly in a straight line instead of flapping back and forth — it would spy over to the east, amid the pine-girt Black Hills, a creek of clapboard cabins called Deadwood City, where human scavengers, too, found plenty of easy pickings. If it flew on its way due north for another 140 miles, pausing, perhaps, to alight on the Devil's Tower it might peer across the rolling prairie to the Big Horn mountains, and the numerous streams and creeks that drained northwards into the mighty Yellowstone. Flapping on further, the crow might well alight on the bank of the broad, if shallow, Powder River.

To most folks this was desolate country where once the Sioux and Cheyenne had roamed, subject to below-zero blizzards or sleet mists for much of the year, the great herds of bison decimated now. Instead, a smattering of hardy homesteaders and cattlemen had moved in to carve out their piece of Montana Territory. One of these was the tall and rangy Randolph McBride, a man as hard, wild and rugged as the land.

Randy, as he was mostly called, was boss of the Leaning Ladder spread on Pumpkin Creek, which ran northwards parallel to the Powder but a long day's ride distant. The creek was an offshoot of the turbulent Tongue River which met the Yellowstone by Miles City.

McBride had, in fact, just returned from trailing more than a thousand head of cattle a hundred miles downstream to Miles City to load onto the new boxcars. He had made a good deal and stashed $5,000 into the 1st National Bank after buying supplies and paying his boys.

Tragedy had struck in his absence. His wife, Rose, was dead, kicked in the throat by her stallion. McBride had dug a six-foot deep grave and invited to the burying what few friends Rose had within travelling distance. He had hammered home a rough wooden cross at the burial spot beneath the shade of some willows along the creek, dug out their battered Bible and read final words of farewell. During the funeral feast he sat like a man in a daze. But his main problem was their 7-year-old son, Matt, who had been bewildered by his mother's death. Luckily, his foreman, or ramrodder, was a solid Mexican, Ramon, whom he had known and trusted for years. His comfortably-padded wife, Maria, had acted as nurse to the boy when Rose was helping him out on the range. She would, at least, help look after Matt well.

Nonetheless, it was a mournful occasion. When the talk was over and their friends gone he felt lonesome, indeed. But he was never one to mope, or find solace in the bottle. He had become inured to much violent death during his years on the frontier and even though Rose's death had hit him hard, too, he was not one to give up easily. So, after kicking his heels around the ranch for a couple of weeks and tidying up his affairs, he decided to ride across to the Powder to see how his nearest neighbour, 'Pop' Williams was making out.

'Come on, Matt,' he called. 'Let's git your pony saddled. Summer's here and a forty-mile ride'll do us the world of good.'

He took it at an easy pace not to tire the boy. But his plan was to raise him to ride and shoot as well as his mother, who had been in her way a bit of a crazy tomboy. The sooner the boy became self-sufficient in the ways of the frontier the better it would be. But what troubled him was how he would handle Matt's schooling. McBride could read and write well enough, himself, but he was by no means acquainted with the latest curriculum. His own education had been how to stay alive, to hunt, fight, survive on the plains and in the mountains among savage nomads.

'At least we ain't got to worry no more about Sioux war parties,' he sang out to the boy as he led the way down through the creek. Not so many years before he would have had to keep alert for the possibility of ambush, of hidden marksmen watching from the high cliff walls. Nonetheless, he still raked the hills, squinting up through narrowed eyelids as the sun began its fall. There were still a few renegade bands around, but mostly lariat Indians more interested in stealing a few cattle or horses than in taking scalps. The bigger danger these days was from no-goods and white scallawags arriving on the Northern Pacific railroad now it had reached Miles City.

The sun had sunk beneath the rim of the plain by the time they trailed into the Williams ranch. The place was strangely quiet, only a smattering of calves and cows to be seen grazing the surrounding prairie and a couple of horses in the corral. There was no smoke rising from the chimney of the cookhouse, no lantern lit, no noise of rowdy cowboys relaxing after a day out on the range.

'Who goes there?' a reedy voice demanded, and old Pop emerged from a stable, a pail of milk in one hand, the other toting a shotgun. 'Is that you, Randy? You got your young un' with you there? Good to see you. Step down and come inside. I ain't got much to offer you, but you're welcome to what I got.'

When they had fed and watered their broncs, rubbed them down from the ride and let them loose in the corral, Randy guided his boy by the shoulder over to the log ranch house.

'Where is everybody?' young Matt whispered, as they climbed onto the veranda. 'Does he live all alone?'

'You'll be wondering what's happened to the boys,' the white-haired old rancher said, as they found him in his untidy kitchen. 'To tell the truth that's what I'm wonderin, too. Tell me, did you see any sign of 'em in Miles City?'

'Nope.' McBride was not long returned from the busy cattle town on the Yellowstone River. 'You sent your herd off 'fore me, didn't you, Pop?'

'Yeah, eight hundred head under my ramrodder Sam Stevens. I thought I could trust that young fella, but it looks like he's done the dirty on me.'

'Maybe that's how he earned the soubriquet Slippery Sam. You think he's absconded with the herd?'

'That's the way it's beginning to

seem. Still, enough of my troubles. You've plenty of your own. I'm sorry I couldn't get over for the burying. Poor Rose. She was a wild, wonderful girl. It hardly seems possible she's gone.'

'Yeah, maybe too wild for her own good. I'd warned her about that stallion, but she would ride him. It was one of those things. A bolt from the blue. Life's a bitch. Just when you think everything's fine and dandy a horse kicks your wife in the head.' Randy gave a shrug of despair as he filled a mug with coffee from a jug on the stove. 'You got a glass of milk for Matt?'

'Sure, I just been struggling with that ornery cow. I have to hogtie her to get at her teats,' Pop said, 'still, at least it was quick. She didn't suffer a lingering death like some wimmin do.'

'Yeah, well, I'd rather we didn't talk about it, if you don't mind, old-timer. We gotta think about tracking down your beeves.'

'Ain't got much in the way of vittles,' Williams wheezed, as he was seized with a coughing fit. 'Cold beef and pickles do you?' He steadied his lean, gnarled frame against a wall while he recovered. 'I'm gittin' old, Randy. There ain't much I can do about it. It looks like they conned me out of most everythang I got. I had to fire the cook, and let the other boys go. I couldn't afford to keep 'em on. Well, there ain't nuthin' for 'em to do now. Of course, I've still got the ranch, but where 'n hell am I gonna git the finance to restock?'

'How many of 'em were there?'

'Sam and Joel Doyle. I guess they were the ring-leaders of the bunch. They had a couple of young hick no-goods along with 'em, Jim Hetherington and Buzz Smith.'

McBride sprawled on a chair at the kitchen-table and sent his Stetson spinning to land on a peg behind the door, making his son chortle. 'When you can do that you'll be a man, my son.'

The boy went to reclaim the hat and give it a try himself. 'Well, they could either have herded them north-west up to Virginia City, which would mean crossing too many rivers and seems doubtful. Or they could have taken the easier option and gone south to Deadwood. The place is packed with miners who'll pay boomtown prices fer beef.'

'Here, get your teeth around this,' Pop said, plonking down wooden platters of sliced beef, along with a pot of Grizzly Bear relish and hunks of sourdough bread. 'Come on, youngster. You must be hungry as a hunter after that long ride. This'll put muscles on them arms of yourn.'

'I already got muscles,' Matt replied, proudly flexing slim biceps. 'See.'

'Gonna be as rootin'-tootin' tough as your pa, eh?'

'No, I don't think I could ever be as tough as him,' the boy said, as he got stuck in. 'This is real tasty, Pop. This relish is real hot. Why do they call you Pop, Pop?'

'Hot as a grizzly ba-ar's breath.' The

old rancher's face creased into a smile. 'I don't rightly know why. Ever since my hair went white folks been calling me Pop.'

He lit a candle in a holder and placed it on the table. 'There, lighten our darkness, oh Lord. Things are gonna be tough now, but we — me and you, too, boy — have gotta git used to being on our ownsome.' He fished his false teeth out of his shirt pocket and munched away with a clacketing sound for some while. 'Sure is a fiery grizzly. I tell you something I *have* got that'll interest your father more. A jug of corn whiskey. I keep it hid in the cellar in case any Sioux turn up. You know, them critters can smell whiskey from twenty miles away and it makes 'em real mean.'

When he had stoked up the tin stove and the boy had gone to bed, he and McBride put up their boots and passed the jug. 'I'm going after 'em,' Randy announced, suddenly. 'I got time on my hands afore the winter sets in. Matt will be fine with Maria and the ranch hands. I'll head for Deadwood soon as I get him home.'

'There ain't no call for you to do that,' Pop protested. 'It ain't your affair. Anyhow, I guess I just gotta accept that my herd has disappeared into thin air.'

'This *is* my affair. Rustling and thieving from my good neighbour is a threat to me. I'll get your herd back or your cash, Pop. Or' — he patted the Remington revolver slung on one hip, his weather-beaten face set grimly — 'there'll be a reckoning between them and me.'

'No! I wish I'd never mentioned this,' Pop protested. 'It'd be a dangfool dangerous thang to do. You got your ranch and the boy to look after. It's no use worrying about an old fool like me. I'd never forgive myself, if — '

'Don't you worry, old-timer.' McBride's lips spread into a wolfish grin. 'I got a hankerin' for some action. I'm goin' after those lousy varmints. Don't argue. Just pass me that jug and wish me luck.'

2

'Hi, yaugh!' Sam Stevens yelled, as he cracked his six-foot stock-whip to urge the leading longhorn steers on along the trail. 'There's Belle Fourche. We're almost there, boys. Keep 'em moving.'

He and his *compadres* had set off from Pop Williams's ranch with the 800-head herd as if intending to go north to Miles City, but once out of sight had forded the Powder River and joined the Deadwood trail. It was simplicity itself, the beeves soon strung out in a long line following the leader. He had put the two young ignorant and ill-nourished cowboys, Jim and Buzz, in the drag to eat their dust. They had even waved gaily to the six-horse stage, loaded with passengers, as it passed.

Joel Doyle, who was riding point on the other side, cut across to him and shouted, 'Don't forget, don't take under eight dollars a head. We need to see a good profit in this.'

His swarthy face beneath the shadow of his wide-brimmed hat split into a grimace of part pleasure, part pain. Joel, his greasy, unwashed clothes covered by a long slicker, was suffering from a bad case of boils on his backside. It came from sitting in a wet saddle for too long, and it made him feel meaner than he normally was. 'All I wanna do is git rid of these friggin' cattle an' sit in a hot tub for months.'

The bellowing cattle had no need to be whipped on now for they had scented water, the Belle Fourche stream, and, with a clashing of horns, had quickened their pace. On the far side could be seen the cabins and ramshackle clapboard houses of the small township nestled twixt plain and mountain. And a tubby gent in a suit and bowler was riding out and kneeing his horse across the river to join them.

'Howdy, boys. Welcome to Belle

Fourche.' His rosy face and blood-stained apron beneath his coat told all they needed to know. He was a butcher and cattle buyer. 'These beeves for sale?'

'If you pay cash they damn sure as hell are.' Sam pulled a hand-written scrap of paper from his shirt pocket. 'They're Forked-Y stock, as you can see from the brands, and this here's authority from Mr Williams to sell.'

'Pop Williams? Is he still alive? How is the old buzzard?'

'He's dang sure fine,' Sam sang out, 'but he's ordered us not to take less than eight dollars a head.'

'Aw, he allus did overprice his stock.' The buyer rode back and forth inspecting the longhorns as they crowded knee-deep into the river to drink. 'I ain't gonna git much for these mangy critters along at Fort Meade, or even up at Deadwood. Best I can offer is five dollars a head, two for the calves.'

'In that case, Fatso, we'll push on up to Deadwood, ourselves,' Joel growled.

'You find beeves someplace else.'

'Don't be like that, boys. You know its a long, hard trail up through the hills to Deadwood City and you won't get more than five dollars there. I'll make it six and three for the calves.'

Joel spat in the river and stared, sourly, as the younger and chippier Sam tried bargaining. But the butcher was adamant. 'Take his offer and go git the cash,' Joel shouted, out of patience. 'Whadda we care. They ain't our cows.'

Some while later Sam came out of the buyer's yard thumbing a wad of $1,000 in greenbacks. He had tucked the other $3,000 in his hat and boots. 'Whoo!' he yelled, tossing two small sacks of gold coin to Jim and Buzz. 'There y'are, boys, I betcha ain't never been paid so well for a short cattle drive. You better thank your lucky stars you met me and Joel.'

'Give Pop my regards and tell him I'm ready to do business with him any day.' The butcher stood and beamed at them as they mounted up and whirled their mustangs eager to depart. 'Hey? Aincha goin' straight back?'

'No.' Sam Stevens tipped a finger to his low-crowned hat and grinned at him. 'We gotta hankerin' to sample the delights of Deadwood City first. He'll get his cash, doncha worry. It's safe with me. And I'll tell him what you say. So long, pal.'

'Yeah,' Joel muttered, as they spurred their broncs away. 'So, where's my share!'

'Two thousand dollars. You'll get it. But don't tell these dumbclucks.' He glanced back at the two scruffy youths who were following along. 'If I were you I would invest it, Joel, like I'm gonna do.'

'Invest it? What you spoutin' about? What in?'

'The roulette wheel, the card tables. There's so many tenderfoot suckers in Deadwood we'll double, no quadruple our take before we pay Pop back.'

'Are you crazy? You really planning on going back to give that silly old fool his money?'

'Sure I am. I ain't a thief. We don't want the law chasin' after us, do we? But first I'm gonna make my fortune by using it as a stake. I'd advise you to do so, too.'

'Partner, just gimme my cash,' Joel growled. ''cause all I'm gonna invest in is whiskey, wimmin and a hot bath. C'mon, let's move.'

*   *   *

'You sure can see why my people claimed this as their sacred hunting ground.' The Buckthorn Kid surveyed the scene before them. Bright sunshine illumined the conifer-clad Black Hills rising to bare granite peaks, amid thickly grassed knolls and deep pools of cold, clear water. 'And why my other people took it off 'em.'

'The reason they took it off 'em was to search for gold.' Della sat her mustang and watched a herd of antelopes grazing in a grove. 'But it sure is fine country. Ain't it time you made up your mind who *are* your people? You can't fight both corners, it'll send you crazy, if you ain't already.'

'You don't understand. My daddy was a big, nasty white trapper up along Snake River. My mammy was one of his five squaws. He whaled me with the buckle of his belt same as he whaled them. He taught me to be hard. The squaws taught me other things. When I was twelve I pulled a knife on him an' told him if he ever raised his belt to me again it would be the last thing he ever did. I rode out and I ain't never seen 'em since. Yeah, I saw early on the best thing for me to do was throw my lot in with the white folks, even though I despise most of 'em.'

'So who would be the exceptions?' Della paused to pull some juicy wild plums and bull berries from the trees. 'Dare I suggest I'm included?'

The Kid grinned at her and ran fingers through his convict crop. 'Some of you — I mean us — are OK! Yeah, I guess I am a tad mixed up about which race I am. As a Sioux I felt bad when they cut off my hair. It was my manhood, my strength. But as a white I thought, 'Aw, hell, what difference does it make?' Come on, let's move.'

They followed the gulch stream that trickled towards Deadwood and soon each side became lined with deep ditches dug by scores of miners who were bent working the gravel placers, pick-axeing, panning or rocking their sluice boxes. They were too busy to pay them much heed.

The town itself was at the junction of the Deadwood and Whitewood creeks and was still defended by a double row of blockhouses which had been built years before to repel the almost daily attacks by desperate Sioux and Cheyenne.

Once through the now unguarded gateway, the Kid and Della rode their horses carefully down the sixty-foot wide street which was lined on either side with pitched-roof cabins, with tents and dug-outs creeping up the sides of the hills; carefully, because it was a chaotic scene of men, women, and children of numerous nationalities, wagons, horses, dogs, mules, oxen, going back and forth.

'You gotta avoid these ditches being dug by miners. You never know when you might tumble into one. Look at that!' the Kid shouted, pointing to bearded men busy as beavers tunnelling beneath the Chinese Celestial Wash House, while next door *The Pioneer* newspaper office was propped up on stilts to prevent its collapse. By miners' law a gold placer could be pursued anywhere regardless of property rights.

'They must be desperate,' Della said, 'to find a new seam.'

'Yeah, it ain't the boom town it used to be. The gold's running out. You wouldn't catch me hacking away down there. I bet they don't find more'n a coupla dollars' worth of dust a day.'

'So, seeing as we ain't got a bean how we gonna eat?'

'Della, you're the horizontal artist. Look at all these randy miners. You can't miss.'

'Aw, I thought there was a catch in it. You told me iffen I helped ya we'd be rich an' I could give up the game.'

'That's true. But we ain't rich yet. Go to it, girl. You'll find me in Number Ten saloon. That's where I gotta meet the man.'

'Who the hell's the man?'

'You'll know him when you see him. Parrot Nose Johnson's the name he gen'rally goes by.'

'How can I tout for business looking like this?' Della shrugged her shoulders, indicating her male garb.

'Tell you what to do, Della: take all your clothes off 'cept for your slicker and boots. Stand down that alleyway, then give a flash as they pass.'

The 19-year-old girl gave a despondent, down-turned grimace. 'Why don't you join me? You give 'em a flash. You might do better than me.'

'Don't talk silly, Della. You go git on with it. Sooner you start, the sooner we eat. Life ain't fair, but that's the way it is if you're a girl.'

'Yes, don't tell me. I know. I got to

capitalize on my natural assets.' The girl hitched her bronc and sauntered away, turning to shout, 'One of these days I might find a decent man and I won't be coming back.'

The Kid grinned and rode on past the stores selling all kinds of imaginable goods from blankets to camp kettles, blasting powder to wagon grease, rubber boots to cans of oysters, or even garden seeds. You name it, they'd got it. He had no qualms about Della's profession. That's the way she was. She would soon make herself a few bucks and probably pick a pocket or two as well. More fool any man who got into her embrace. They had only their lust to blame. She was an expert. She would fleece them like they were lambs.

So, to tide him over until they were flush, he sold the ill-tempered mustang for twenty dollars, and sauntered into the crowded No. 10 saloon. It was a long, smoky, spit-and-sawdust place, dimly lit by bacon grease lamps, the only *aperitifs* coming from big barrels of Dutchman's beer or Irishman's whiskey. Miners were crowded around a battered roulette table; its wheel rarely ceased turning, night and day. Others were engrossed in games of three-card monte, keno, faro or poker. They wagered wildly, tossing down pouches of gold dust. But most of the profit went to the house, or to the more sober professional gamblers lured to Deadwood looking for easy pickings.

'I must look like some damn hick,' Buckthorn muttered as he leaned against a wall and supped at a mug of beer that had cost him ten cents. He was highly self-conscious of his ill-fitting jacket and ugly shoes. But maybe he could capitalize on that by playing the idiot and try a few card tricks of his own. 'Howdy, gents,' he said, giving a goofy grin and easing himself into a spare seat at a table. 'Mind if I join the game? Maybe you could explain to me how I play?'

Sam Stevens had thrown away his filthy garments, soaked in a hot tub, fitted himself out with a four-button suit, linen shirt with celluloid collar, gold watch and stickpin in his cravat, polished boots and a curly-brimmed Stetson. A 'capillary manipulator' had trimmed and crimped his hair, splashed him liberally with perfume, and even waxed and twirled his moustache ends. Sam had strutted along the sidewalk like a rooster, intent on painting the town red.

As he passed an alleyway he saw a young girl leaning against a wall, one shapely bare leg protruding from her rubberized slicker. She gave him a toothy grin. 'Got two dollars to spare, handsome? I'll make it worth your while.'

'Sure, why not?' Sam glanced furtively around but nobody was interested in him. He dived into the alley and found she was stark naked beneath her coat. In a jiffy he had her legs up around his waist as she clawed and clung to him like a demented cat . . .

So, Sam was feeling pretty pleased

with himself when he entered No. 10 Saloon, bought a half-pint glass of Irish, and joined a game of stud poker. When the clown of a 'breed in his too-tight coat asked them to explain the game he could hardly believe his luck. 'Sure, buddy,' he said, lighting a cigar, and winking across at the swarthy Joel Doyle. 'We'll show you the ropes. How much cash you got?'

'Twenty bucks,' the Kid replied, with an eager grin. 'Just sold my hoss. I'm lookin' to git lucky.'

'Yeah,' Joel growled, dealing the pack, 'it might just be your lucky day. Where'd you get that haircut? Somebody use blunt shears?'

'It's the latest fashion for 'breeds,' Sam sneered. 'Didn'tcha know?'

'I ain't a 'breed. My daddy was a white man. Buck Thorn. You heard of him?'

'Nope, so who was your mammy? Or don't you know?'

'Come on, boys, quit it. You're s'posed to be teaching me this game.

What do I do next?'

'Put your cash in the pot,' Sam instructed, in his dandyish way. 'Now let me see your hand. Diamonds, eh? You try an' get a couple more. You might win.'

'Am I s'posed to let you see my cards?'

'We've got to teach you, haven't we?'

Joel had soaked his boils in hot suds, but his only outlay in the gents' outfitters had been new red flannel long johns, with a trapdoor. He had always been careful with his cash and was not used to being rich. He had pulled back on his cowhide pants, worn canvas shirt, big bandanna, and weatherbeaten boots. They had grown creased and comfortable on his muscular frame. Why change them? Or his hat? It took time to knock a Stetson into a good shape and his greasy headpiece looked right and rarely left his head.

They played a while, the Kid losing most of his cash, affecting to be puzzled by proceedings. But then he suddenly began to win. 'Three picture cards,' he exclaimed, producing a Jack, Queen and King. 'That means I win, don't it?'

'Of course it does,' an onlooker said, who was watching the game. A couple of other burly, bearded miners had gathered round to see what was going on. 'Go on, kid, you're on a run.'

Joel flipped out cards again, growling malevolently, 'You sure you never played this game before?'

The Kid shook his head. 'Never. Must be beginner's luck.'

Suddenly it was Sam's turn to start losing while the young 'breed had not only won back his losses but was fast adding to his stake. He bit his lip, nervously, and reached into his back pocket for more cash. 'Hey, my wallet's gone!' He half got to his feet, frantically searching his other pockets. 'Hot damn! I had a hundred dollars in it. I've been robbed.'

One of the miners commiserated. 'You gotta keep your hand on your poke in this town, pal.'

Sam sat down again. 'Lend me fifty, Joel.'

The Kid noticed, as Sam opened his jacket, that he had a brand new, pearl-handled Smith & Wesson, shoulder hung. What was this dude, he wondered, some kind of shootist? He would have to step carefully.

They played for another two hours, Buckthorn expressing his surprise as he won consistently. Rotgut whiskey and his anger at being robbed made Sam Stevens throw wild. When the down-at-heel, dark-eyed half-Indian produced two Jacks and an Ace kicker it was the last straw.

'I gotta be calling it a night,' the Kid drawled, leaning forward to scoop up the pot of more than ninety dollars.

'Oh, no you don't,' Sam snapped. 'Hold it right there you lousy cheating 'breed.'

'That ain't a word I like.' Buckthorn froze, his hands cupped around the cash. His lips curled back over his white teeth in a taunting smile. 'No need to get nasty, boys. I'll give ya a chance tomorrow to win it back. But I gotta hit the hay. I didn't get no sleep last night.'

'How did you arrive by that Ace, boy?' Joel demanded. 'It's my opinion you ain't been playing fair and square. If you take my advice, 'breed, you'll get your arse out of this saloon forthwith. You can leave that cash.'

'Yeah,' Sam added, producing the S & W with a flourish to aim at him. 'I've allus wanted to shoot me a redskin. So you better not come back.'

The Kid straightened up, his fingers spread towards the ancient rusty revolver stuffed in his belt. 'That's a classy shooter you got there, mister. I ain't a match for that. But that cash is mine and I ain't walking out of here without it.'

'Is that a fact?' Joel scuffed his chair back to grip the walnut butt of his own Colt .45. 'You ain't going nowhere, boy.'

'I wouldn't bet on that.' The saloon had fallen silent, even the professor of piano ceasing his discordant jangle, as miners moved back out of the line of fire. The fourth voice rang out confidently. 'I'd leave them shooting irons if I were you.'

The crowd turned to see a beady-eyed gent, with a prominent, whiskey-reddened nose, clad in a red and orange checked suit and brown derby who had entered the saloon and was now standing ten feet away holding a peculiar shotgun with three barrels aimed at Sam and Joel.

'Don't make a move,' he shouted, 'just do as I say or it'll be the last move you make. I'll blast you both to hell.'

Sam and Joel, small arms half-drawn, were taken aback by his sudden appearance. No man cared to back a pistol against a shotgun at close range, not one as menacing in style as that held by a man of obvious iron nerve.

'This ain't none of your business,' Sam whined. 'That boy's cheated us.'

'That boy's a friend of mine. Maybe you tried to cheat him.' The red-nosed dude had his finger curled around the first of three triggers. 'This Dickson's this year's state of the art from Edinburgh. Finest shotgun ever made. It's got automatic ejectors so it's fast. And it packs two-and-a-half-inch shells so it's gonna blow your heads clean off and one more barrel to spare if I miss.'

'Where'd you get that thang?' Joel muttered.

'If it's any of your business, which it ain't, I won it off some English aristocrat back along the trail. He assured me it's deadly accurate, so if I were you two I'd take them guns out real slow with two fingers and pass them across. OK?'

Sam tensed, debating silently whether to draw, spin and shoot. He met Joel's murky eyes and shrugged, placing the S & W carefully down on the card table. Surlily Joel clattered his Colt across, too. 'There'll be another day,' he growled.

The Buckthorn Kid scooped up his

winnings and began stuffing the crumpled notes into his pockets. 'Thanks, boys. Mighty nice playing with you. Howdy, Mr Johnson. I been waiting for you.'

'I just stepped off the stage. Might have known I'd find you in trouble. Come on, Kid. We'll leave these miserable rats in their nest, and find somewhere more congenial.'

'Howdy, Della.' The Kid grinned some more as the girl, back in her male attire, burst into the saloon. 'How's it going? This here's Parrot Nose . . . I mean Mr Johnson.'

'That's her!' Sam screamed out and pointed an accusing finger. 'That's the skinny, buck-toothed bitch who stole my wallet.'

'What's he talkin' about?' Della screeched. 'I ain't never set eyes on him afore.'

'You been making some nasty accusations, mister,' Johnson called out, the twenty-four-inch barrels of the twelve gauge still aimed unerringly at them. 'You got any proof?'

'No, 'course he ain't,' Buckthorn said. 'Calling me a cheat. I oughta kill him for that. What a cheek.' He picked up the Smith & Wesson. 'Mm, nice piece. I think I'd better confiscate this. Della, you can have the Colt.'

This was too much for Joel who, with a howl of wrath, raised his gnarled fists to make a grab at the Kid. But Sam held him back. 'Aw, forget it, Joel. What's a few greenbacks? We got plenty more where they come from. Maybe he did win it straight after all.'

'Good thinkin', pal.' The Kid spun the S & W on a finger with practised ease. 'I allus wanted to try one of these self-cockers. If you're so flush maybe we can meet again for another game?'

Sam shrugged, and took another swig from his jug of whiskey. 'Get lost,' he said. 'And take that poxy doxie with you.'

When the three had gone he stood meeting the baleful eyes of the miners. 'What you all staring at? They had the drop on us. What did you want? Blood?'

He hurled the jug at the pot-bellied stove, smashing it and making a cloud of flame leap out. 'Come on, Joel. I'm hungry. Let's go eat.'

They wandered back to the Grand Central hotel, Joel cursing at the way they had been robbed and humiliated into the bargain. 'I'll kill that damn 'breed,' he vowed, 'one of these days.'

Sam paused to get some more cash out of his filthy long johns which he had hidden beneath the straw of his horse's stall in the livery. He made a pretence of seeing that the mustang was being well cared for.

'We've got plenty. We'll recoup our losses.'

They had booked into the hotel's best room. Not that there was much choice. It was a hive of plank-partitioned cubicles above the stables. Then they filled their bellies with roast duck and cherries, followed by plum pie, in the dining-room.

Joel was still seething. 'How we gonna get even with them three?'

'I dunno,' Sam mused, lighting another Havana. 'I got a feeling that Parrot Nose is a professional. It might be best to stay on the right side of them.'

3

Randolph McBride cinched tight the heavy, high-pommelled Denver saddle on the feisty stallion, Satan, whose kick had killed his wife. He needed some strong handling to get him out of his stall and to get aboard, but he resisted the urge to take out his resentment on the half-wild brute. Many a man would have whipped, restrained with ropes, cruelly spurred, or, at the very least, twisted his ear, to get his submission. But McBride wasn't a man like that. He looked for partnership in a horse, even friendship and respect. With such a snorting, prancing, kicking beast, that possibility seemed remote, indeed.

He hardly had time to shout goodbye to his son, and Ramon and Maria, who stood watching, steering the stallion by sheer strength around the ranch yard, then making a rush to clear a five-barred gate, and away, hanging on like grim death. Satan was aptly named.

Talk about acceleration. The stallion whooshed away like a ball from a cannon. McBride gave him his head for twenty miles in a wild ride down Pumpkin Creek, first at a gallop then at an erratic lope, scattering cattle, kicking up turves, swerving past rocks and splashing through streams. When the black finally slowed down, frothing at the jaws and sweat-lathered, his rider eased him in and leaned forward to pat his strong neck.

'There y'are, boy. You ain't gonna git me off your back,' he crooned. 'I'm here to stay, but I ain't gonna hurt you.'

He carefully stepped down, keeping a tight hold on the reins, took a rag from his blanket pack, wetted it in the stream and washed the horse down. He took a break to boil up some coffee, then walked the horse for a bit, turning his back to him, and was glad to note that the stallion followed him along without resistance, almost docilely. After a couple of miles he let him drink, gave him a sugar lump, swung into the saddle and went on his way. If they kept up a steady lope they might do another forty miles before nightfall.

'Don't worry,' he told the horse. 'It weren't your fault you killed her. It was one of those things that happen. An accident. We gotta put it behind us. I'm your new boss now.'

The stallion waggled his ears and gave a high-pitched whinny as he stepped along. Whether he understood or not, the horse obviously felt good being out and on the move under the wide Montana skies. And so did the man.

McBride had decided to go across country to the Black Hills, rather than take the easy route along the trail to Belle Fourche. There were rivers to ford and ravines to cross, and he would have to find his way through the thickly wooded hills, but he figured it was the faster option. Time was of the essence because Sam Stevens and his sidekicks had at least two weeks start on him. It was a mistake he would regret.

It was by no means certain they had headed for Deadwood. It was just a hunch McBride had. He hoped to cut them off. The element of surprise would help. He was confident he could handle the two rustlers, Sam Stevens and the older man, Doyle. The two teenagers shouldn't be any trouble. But there was, of course, always the element of danger. You never knew what a gun-crazy kid might do.

When he left the southern limit of Pumpkin Creek he headed on across the prairie, which had greened over after the long winter, shimmering now like a wind-rippled sheet of silk. By early evening he arrived at the middle reaches of the great Powder River not far from where Two Moon's village had been wiped out by the cavalry. He made camp beneath some willows along the bank. The river was murky and alkali so he used water from his canteen, and soon had a small fire blazing and his coffee pot bubbling. He fed the stallion some split corn, hobbled his back hoofs with his woven-rawhide lariat, chewed on a strip of beef jerky himself, and leaned back to rest against his saddle, always keeping his seven-shot Spencer carbine close to hand and the Remington revolver in his belt-holster at half-cock.

The sun was bleeding away onto the crags of the Big Horn range, briefly setting the night sky aglow. McBride pulled off his boots, made them secure beneath his saddle, threw a log on the fire, crawled into his soogan, lit his pipe, and watched the stars slowly appear one by one. The only sound was of the horse chomping the grass, the ceaseless wind, sometimes seeming to carry voices, and the distant howl of a coyote. Living so close to nature, McBride could easily understand how the Indian tribes believed so strongly in the supernatural. The image of his wife's face and eyes crossed his mind, but it didn't do to linger on her. He tugged his hat down over his nose, hunched himself more comfortably into his topcoat, and drifted into sleep. It had been a strenuous day.

He was on his way again before first light, fording the Powder and heading east towards the Little Powder stream. He rode deep in the saddle, the Spencer slung across his back, going with the rhthym of the stallion, letting him pick his own route and speed, guiding him steadily south along the river's edge.

The only sign of humanity he encountered were occasional knots of buffalo hunters, if you could call those smelly, hairy, lice-ridden creatures human. They camped in dug-outs with their carts and powerful rifles out in the middle of the great northern plain, sometimes slaughtering 100 bison in a stand, slicing away the robes and leaving the rest, great lumps of red, raw flesh to rot. At four dollars a hide it was profitable work.

McBride gave them a wave and rode on, even though they seemed to want him to stop and talk. There were still herds of buffalo about. Those of the southern plain were all but gone. Soon those of the north would suffer the same fate if the relentless shooting went on. He could not condemn them. He had done his share of hunting. But a man had to have a strong stomach to indulge in this wholesale slaughter.

Nonetheless, he paused to pull his big Bowie and slice a hump and a chunk of tongue from a bull that had been brought down earlier that day, the flies already buzzing over the body. He washed the meat in the stream, stuffed it in his canvas 'warbag', slung it from the saddle horn, and went on his way.

The ones to really suffer, of course, had been the nomadic tribes who roamed the central plains and depended on the bison for most of their needs. Towards high noon he spied a small band of these camped in a huddle of tattered tipis by the stream. For reasons of their own they had left the reservation, but, as he approached, he saw they were a far cry from the proud, flamboyant warriors of a few years before. They were a defeated race, strangers in their own land.

'Howdy!' he called, raising his hand in the peace sign and riding across in a semi-circle to their camp. Ragamuffin children and barking curs ran to regard him, squaws huddled in rags looked up from their smoky fires, but there was a look of both fear and curiosity in their eyes.

Two men in traditional buckskins, their long black hair sheathed in otter skins, necklaces tight around their throats, were attending to their painted ponies in a corral and turned to watch him with hostility, one reaching for a lance.

But an old man, his face wizened, huge ear-rings dangling to his shoulders, rose from his place by the fire, his blanket draped around him, and walked to meet him. McBride noted from his beaded moccasins that he was a Hunkpapa Sioux, the same tribe as Sitting Bull.

'You wan' something, mister?' he asked, suspiciously.

'Nope.' Randy McBride grinned at him, surpised he could speak some English. 'Just passing by.' He reached in his warbag and pulled out the chunk of raw hump. 'This any good to you?' He tried some Siouan of his own. '*Wash-tay*. Good.'

'Sure.' The old man squinted up at him through narrowed eyes as one of the squaws went forward to receive the gift. 'You come smoke?'

'Yeah, I could do with a break.' McBride figured if these were lariat Indians, or horse-stealers, it might be best to befriend them, or, at least, let them know he was well armed. He didn't want them following him; these boys could sneak a horse away from under your nose. Already the men at the corral had pricked up their attention and wandered across to eye the big stallion, enviously.

Satan hitched securely to a nearby cottonwood stump, McBride squatted down by the old man's fire. He took out his pipe and pouch of tobacco, tipping out a generous handful and offering it to the Indian. It wasn't polite in those parts to enquire too closely about the antecedents of either white or red man, but the old man volunteered the information.

'Me scout at Fort Keogh . . . after Bighorn.'

'You fight at Bighorn?'

'Maybe.' Man-on-Hill, as he called himself, smiled, craftily. 'Me scout Gen-lal Clook.'

'Crook? He's a good man.'

'Yuh. Glood man. You army man?'

'No.' McBride lit up and puffed his pipe. 'I was in Deadwood when Custer cashed in his chips. That was what, eight years ago?'

'Clips?' The old guy passed his own long-stemmed pipe across so McBride did a swap. 'What clips?'

'Chips? Oh' — he did sign language of his own, thumb across throat and making a croak — 'When Yellow Hair died.'

'Ey-hee! *Wama nuncha*. Chief of thieves.'

They chatted for a while until Satan began snorting and rearing, flailing his forehoofs, trying to pull free. 'What's the matter with him?' McBride jumped up and tried to calm the stallion as the Indians began to laugh.

'You lend him?' The old man had got up stiffly to sweep his arm towards a somewhat stunted mare in the corral. He made a fist of his arm. '*Washtay! Good!*'

'So, that's what's the matter with him. She's in season, is she? That mare's a bit small for him. But, why not? I won't charge no stud fees.'

The young Sioux whooped and threw their own lariats over Satan's neck, guiding the kicking, whinnying stallion into the corral. Everybody gathered round to cheer as the mare raised her tail and the arch-necked horse stiffened and reared over her.

'Well, that should quieten him down for a bit,' McBride said as, afterwards, they dragged the powerful stallion from the corral. 'Maybe we'll meet again one day and you'll be riding his son or daughter.'

By now the the hump was baked 'crumpy' on the outside and tender within. 'All it needs is a dusting of cinnamon,' McBride said as he devoured a slice. He tossed a few silver coins to the children, climbed back on the stallion, shouted, 'So long, you all,' and pounded on his way.

'Well, that was a nice li'l interval, weren't it, boy?' he shouted. 'I guess we must be headin' into Wyomin' by now.'

As the great red ball of sun began its fast fall again he sighted the Devil's Tower, the column of rock rising from the plain which, in the past, a half-naked warrior would climb to pray on its peak and sing out to his *wyakin* spirit guide. Beyond were the 2000-feet high mountains, the shadowy Black Hills.

'We'll camp here tonight,' he said.

'By tomorrow night we oughta be in Deadwood.'

⋆   ⋆   ⋆

He was rudely awakened in the cold light of dawn by the hard prod of octagonal iron to his brow and, coming to his senses, squinted along the 30-inch barrel of a Sharps 'Old Reliable'. A wizened face beneath a floppy-brimmed hat peered down at him. 'Don't make a move, mister. This trigger's light as a feather. One touch'll blow you to blazes.'

'I believe you,' McBride muttered, staying where he was. 'Whadda you want?'

'You got his Spencer, Charlie?' drawled the old man, whose stench proclaimed him to be a buff'-hunter. He wore an overlarge overcoat, once black but now sheened to zinc green by time, belted by a bit of rope.

'Sure have,' Charlie whined. 'And his knife' — McBride had stuck it in the turf close by — 'he's jest a toothless dog now. He ain't got no bite.'

'Don't be so sure about that. He's got a revolver under that soogan someplace. We gonna have to deal with that. But, first, while you got your hands free, mister, jest pass me them boots from behind your head. I figure that's where you keep your cash, eh? Nice 'n' easy, now.'

McBride glanced past them to a spot on the plain 100 yards away where they had left their mustangs and a two-wheeled, small cart in order to creep up on him. Satan was hobbled fifty feet away. Another hunter, a skinny varmint in a coonskin cap, was toting an ancient Henry rolling block rifle, and grinning, gap-toothed, at him. All in all, his chances didn't look good.

'Don't try nuthin', mister. This hyar's .45–120 calibre with a kick like a mule.' The old man held the twenty-pound Sharps rifle as if it was as light as a feather. 'It'll blow your head off.'

'You win.' McBride carefully reached

behind and handed over his boots. They were empty. His roll of greenbacks was, in fact, stuffed in the tops of his long woollen socks. 'Help yourselves.'

'Charlie, take a look.'

'Ain't nuthin' here,' the wolfish-looking fellow replied, feeling inside. 'That stallion's worth two-hundred dollars. He must have cash someplace.'

'Yep. You better git on your feet, mister. Keep your hands high. Step out of ya bag.'

McBride did so, tempted to pull back his topcoat and go for his Remington. It would be his only chance, but he knew it would be suicidal for the smelly old guy now had the Old Reliable stuck in his midriff. 'You can have my wallet, boys, an' we'll say no more about this. But you cain't take my horse. That'd be a dastardly thing to do.'

'Aw, kill him now,' Charlie shouted. 'What we hanging about for?'

'I got friends up north,' the rancher warned. 'You do that they'll hunt you down and hang you all. You can have my wallet and go on your way. I got plenty in the bank. I'll open my coat and bring it out, shall I?'

'Slowly,' the old buff'-hunter muttered, obviously wondering if McBride was telling the truth. 'One false move you're a dead man.'

'Dead men tell no tales,' the 'coonskin cap one growled. 'You kill him, Seth, or I will.'

'Easy, boys,' McBride whispered, opening his coat. If he went for his revolver there and then would he have a chance . . . ? It was now or never.

Suddenly, however, there was a hiss through the air of an arrow that thudded into the old man's back. 'Aargh!' he cried. McBride pushed the barrel of the Sharps away as it kicked and boomed out, the bullet crashing past his head.

'Coonskin panicked, spinning around to face three feathered Indians who had appeared as if from nowhere on their ponies. He fired his old Henry too fast and to no effect and a lance whistled through the air to embed in his chest, toppling him onto his back.

Fast as a whisper, McBride whipped out his six-gun, cocked it with a gloved hand, and fired in one fluid, unerring motion as Charlie turned, too, and aimed the Spencer at the Sioux. McBride's bullet spun him in his tracks, and he expired with a groan as he collapsed.

Man-on-the-Hill grinned at him as he rode up. 'Hey, like old times, yah?' The two young braves were on their ponies beside him.

'Yeah, but maybe you better not scalp 'em.'

'No!' 'Coonskin was clutching the shaft of the lance, its iron point embedded in his chest. 'Please,' he cried in terror. 'Don't let 'em!'

The older hunter was lying face down, still alive, trying to grope at the arrow in his back. 'Waal, I'm damned,' he groaned.

'Never a truer word spoken.' McBride gritted his teeth and put a bullet into the back of his head. It was like dispatching a wounded bull. He felt no other remorse. Better than a lingering death at the hands of the Sioux.

'No,' 'Coonskin pleaded, his thin jaws agonized. 'We weren't gonna kill you. Please — '

McBride gave him the same *coup de grace*, putting the seven-inch barrel of the Remington between his eyes this time. The explosion crashed out and blood spurted from the hole.

Before a man could barely say die three men were dead, toppled like lifeless trees. There was only the brimstone reek of drifting gunsmoke. He turned away with a grimace of disgust from the necessary task.

'How about some coffee, boys?' McBride kept his revolver cocked and hanging from his hand for it occurred to him that they, too, might have been intent on robbing him. 'Where in tarnation did you come from?'

The two Hunkpapa warriors were

intent upon searching the rancid bison-killers for anything of value and examining their rifles. Man-on-the-Hill turned his pony and jogged away to inspect the small cart hauled by one of their mustangs. When McBride walked over to join him, the old Indian was going through the supplies. There was gunpowder, lead, brass shells, primers, skinning knives and a portable grindstone.

Man-on-the-Hill hailed him with a grunt of contentment as he pointed to sacks of flour, baking powder, dried apples, pinto beans, coffee beans and a side of bacon. He stuck his finger into a can of molasses and sucked at it. 'This good.'

'Yeah, but that ain't.' McBride examined a large bottle marked poison. 'Strychnine. Looks like they were after wolves, too. This give you bad belly-ache. Dead in hour or two.' He smashed the bottle on a rock and watched the poison seep away into the mud. 'Them low-down hyenas knew a trick or two. I've a mind you'd agree they're a breed of black-hearted devils who are better off dead.'

When they had stirred up the fire and breakfasted on bacon, biscuits and coffee, Man-on-the-Hill explained in his broken English and by liberal use of sign-language that they had come to Devil's Tower as a pilgrimage to pray to the spirits. '*Wanagi yata*.' Place of souls.

'Lucky for me you did,' McBride said. 'Otherwise it'd be me lying there dead, not them. I'd like to thank you boys. If you're ever passing my ranch, the Leaning Ladder, on the Pumpkin, you call in, you hear? But, meanwhile, what we gonna do with these stiffies?'

Man-on-the-Hill directed his two warriors to drag the corpses into the jumble of rocks at the foot of the tower and cover them up with rubble. After they had spoken with the spirits they would, he said, take the mustangs and cart back to their camp.

'Right,' the rancher said, saddling the

stallion. 'Then go back to the reservation. Skeddadle! You savvy? It ain't safe for you to hang around. If the mates of these varmints hear what's happened they'll be lookin' for vengeance.' He slung the Spencer over his back, tied his soogan and warbag behind the saddle and swung aboard. 'I gotta be on my way. It's been good knowing you. Thanks again.'

'It was not us, it was spirits who guarded you.' Man-on-the-Hill's solemn face cracked into a smile. 'You are good man. Go, McBride.'

4

Parrot Nose Johnson shuffled the deck with nimble fingers as the main game in No 10 Saloon split up and he watched Sam Stevens lurch towards the door, $500 dollars or so the poorer. 'There's never been a truer maxim that a fool and his money are quickly parted,' he said, counting his winnings and passing his share to Buckthorn. 'That bird was ripe for plucking.'

'He don't seem to care none.' The Kid was resplendent in shiny black leather jacket and pants, supple black boots from which Mexican spurs jingled, a blue polka-dot bandanna and a new, high-crowned black hat, silver conchos decorating its band. 'He's spending greenbacks 'n' gold like there's no tomorrow.'

Johnson, in his florid check suit, stroked his moustache beneath his prominent nose, raised a tumbler of redeye and asked, 'Do you think he'd be any use to us? We'll be needin' four or five more guns.'

'Well, he certainly ain't honest. The whisper is that cash him and his pal are frittering away ain't rightly theirs to spend. It belongs to some rancher whose beeves they sold. In my opinion, Mr Johnson, they're amateurish and incompetent.'

'I ain't expectin' them to do any thinkin',' Parrot Nose growled. 'I'm the one who does that. All I want is some boys to tote guns, put the frighteners on the railroad men. Doncha worry, Kid, you and I will split the biggest share. This is going to be big, believe me.'

Parrot Nose was sitting in a high-backed chair in the saloon corner where, eight years before, William Butler Hickok presided over the poker game while to the north 30,000 Sioux and Cheyenne fought for survival against the US Army. Why the legend-ary gun-fighter had chosen one day to invite sudden death by sitting with his back to the door was still something of a mystery.

'If you think they've got the nerve I'll sound them out,' the Kid remarked, getting to his feet, and glancing around at the room full of half-drunken miners. 'We certainly ain't got a lot of choice among these dipsoes and deadbeats.'

He paused and put a hand on the older man's shoulder. 'Are you sure your information is the real thing?'

'Sure I'm sure this time,' Johnson blustered, refilling his glass from the bottle. 'It ought to be. I spent enough cash bribing the railroad superintendent at Bismark. We've got to be moving out soon, so tell those two to make their minds up one way or the other.'

★ ★ ★

Sam Stevens was having the time of his life. Every day was like Thanksgiving. He was living like a lord: fat turkey

70

dinners, best bourbon, fancy cigars, and a different gal on his arm, morning, noon and nighttime. Prairie nymphs, soiled doves, calico queens, painted cats, call 'em what you like, there was no shortage. In a town teeming with hundreds of single men with gold dust in their pokes it meant that none of the goodtime gals was, with aid of paint and padding, too old or ugly to make a living.

Variety was the spice of life so this night Sam was escorting a whore renowned for her wildness and debauchery, Tattooed Nell. He paid for the best seats in a box hanging over the stage at the Deadwood Academy of Music, high-falutinly called, which was packed out for a performance by Miss Violet de Montmorency, the Queen of Song, as she was billed, 'prior to her departure for Europe to perform before crowned heads.'

Nell, in a clinging green velvet dress, which revealed a vast tattooed bosom draped with paste jewellery, was in high spirits after being treated by Sam to a seven-course meal, wine and whiskey. She planned to get her sticky fingers on more of her consort's cash before the night was through.

Whistles and applause for Miss Violet dimmed somewhat when the curtains opened to reveal beyond the footlight flares a lady much older, beneath rouge and powder, than expected. As she curtsied and twittered, Tattooed Nell yelled out, 'She's old enough to drop them teeth into a glass of water!'

A burst of laughter mingled with cries of 'Shame' and 'Give the singer a chance', but it was obvious the loud and flushed Nell was going to be the star attraction.

Miss Violet went into some high-pitched and discordant operatic renderings, until Nell bawled out, 'What you trying to do, sister, lay an egg?'

'Really!' Miss Violet threw her hands up to quell the noise. 'In all my illustrious career I've never been so insulted.'

'Hang around, honey, I only just begun. Where'd you learn to sing? In a cathouse? Why don't you relieve our eardrums and go git on that ship across the Atlantic. The sooner the better.'

'I demand that woman be ejected from the theatre,' Miss Violet shrieked, pointing at her.

'Jest let anybody try,' Nell yelled, pulling a revolver from her handbag. 'It's you who's gonna be dejected.' She began blamming away wildly, bullets whistling and thudding into the stage around the artiste, who burst into tears and fled.

'There y'are, folks,' Nell beamed. 'Did y'all a favour. Bring on the next act. Don't forget, drinks are on Sam here in the interval. He's real flush.'

'I ain't that flush,' Sam said, trying to extricate himself from her clutches. 'I've been having a bad time at the tables. Aw, come on, Nell, let's git you outa here 'fore you shoot somebody.'

★　★　★

'When are you going to bring an end to this lawlessness, Governor?'

73

'What do you mean?' The Governor of Wyoming was sitting behind his big desk in his office at Cheyenne and glowering at the pasty-faced reporter from *The Plainspeaker*.

'That was your election pledge. How did a dangerous bank and train robber manage to blow a hole in the wall of the guardhouse at Fort Laramie? Have you any clues yet?'

'He blew a hole in the wall with dynamite smuggled into him by an accomplice, Della Reid.'

'How did she do that? Why wasn't she searched?'

'She *was* searched. Her bag was. She had the dynamite hidden under her skirt.' The governor blew smoke across at the young journalistic upstart in his cheap suit, with his pencil poised over his notebook. 'You don't expect my officers to delve into every female visitor's drawers, do you?'

'Couldn't you employ female guards? Della Reid, as you know yourself, has been convicted for prostitution, forgery, pick-pocketing, passing counterfeit cash, harbouring a criminal, et al. She was a known accomplice of the Buckthorn Kid. Shouldn't your men have kept an eye on her?'

'Of course they kept an eye on her.' Who did this poky-nosed whippersnapper think he was? Where did he get his nerve? the governor wondered. 'We have the situation under control.'

'But you haven't arrested them?' the reporter prompted. 'Why was the Buckthorn Kid sprung from jail? Doesn't it indicate that he might be planning another big robbery?'

'That's a possibility, sure. We have alerted all law officers in Wyoming to be on the lookout for these two abscondees. We have advised Wells Fargo and the Central Pacific railroad company to increase their safety precautions if any large sums are to be transported.'

'Yes, but the Kid wrecked a train and nearly got away with ten thousand dollars last time. Couldn't he strike again?'

'No, I don't believe so. He was

working with a ruthless gang of outlaws before. Most of whom have now been killed or are in prison serving long terms. He was just a small cog in the wheel, albeit the one who used the explosives. He didn't succeed then and he's unlikely to do so again.'

'You have no idea where he might be? What if he's gone north to Dakota or Montana?'

'We've thought of that. It's not my territory, but I have advised the new Northern Pacific railroad to tighten their security and be on the *qui vivre*.' The governor suddenly exploded with anger, thumping his fist on his desk. 'Come off it, sonny. These are just two small-time crooks on the lam. Don't you think I've got more to do with my time than worry about them? That's off the record. This interview is over. Get the hell out of here.'

'Your reaction suggests to me you might — '

The governor hurled a book at the cub reporter. 'Get out!'

'Whew!' Joel held his nose as Sam Stevens emerged from the barber shop. 'You stink like a French hooer. You been havin' your moustache twirled again?'

'You gotta look the part if you're gonna play poker with the high-rollers, Joel,' Sam replied, primly. 'Do you think Wyatt Earp, when he was here, went around looking like an out-of-work cowpoke? There's a big game on.'

'Big game,' Joel scoffed. 'We've lost near on two thousand dollars and spent the rest. You ain't never gonna win enough to pay back Pop Williams. Anyhow, he'll be dead soon so who cares? But I say it's time we moved on 'fore some lawman comes lookin' for us.'

'Maybe you're right.' Sam looked despondent as he fiddled with the stud of his celluloid collar. 'These dang things!' he tore it off and hurled it across the street. 'I only got a coupla hundred left, Joel. How about you?'

'Not much more. Come on, pal. We'll git our broncs and mosey on. We'll find another job someplace.'

'No!' Sam protested. 'I ain't goin' back to poking cows. Thirty dollars a month all found? Pah! I'd rather rob the Deadwood stage.'

They sat down on the steps of the sidewalk as the two down-at-heel teenagers, Buzz Smith and Jim Hetherington, came across to join them. 'Having a good time, boys?' Sam asked.

'All my cash has gone on monte and whiskey and some damn wildcat gal who ran off as soon as my winnings was spent,' Buzz complained. 'Can you loan us a grubstake, Sam? We're broke.'

'No, I can't. You've had your cash,' Sam shouted, but then relented. 'Aw, hell, I know what it's like to be raised poor as a buzzard in a boneyard. Here y'are.' He scraped a handful of grubby notes from his pocket. 'That's about half of what I got. Looks like I come to the end of Pop's cash.' He was unaware that the Kid and Della were standing behind, listening.

'What we gonna do, Sam?' Jim asked.

'Hell knows.'

'Howdy, boys.' The Buckthorn Kid stepped down to sit beside them. 'Why y'all looking so down in the dumps?'

'You know why,' Joel growled, ''cause that friend of yourn skinned us of what was ourn.'

'Just to show there's no hard feelings,' the Kid said, presenting the fine Smith & Wesson to Sam, 'you can have this back. I don't go much on these double actions: you're inclined to fire off your whole six in a frenzy. Me, I like to thumb a gun myself. It gives a man time to think, to pick his shot. I got me a nice li'l Allen and Hopkins .32. Suits me fine.'

Joel eyed the S & W, enviously. 'What about my Colt?'

'Sure, give him it back, Della. We'll git you something else. Now, boys, did I hear you say you was broke? Would you be interested in making a pile of cash?'

'Doing what?' Sam asked, suspiciously.

'Robbing a train, that's what. I ain't talking peanuts. This is big. Your take would be ten thou'.'

'Ten thousand?' Buzz squealed with disbelief. 'Are you serious?'

'Keep your voice down. Don't tell the whole town. That's ten thou' between you. Are you in or out?'

Old before their time with rotting teeth and constant colds, Buzz and Jim looked at each other and the latter hooted, 'Jeez, count us in!'

'Hang on a minute.' As usual, Joel looked as if his boils were still paining him. 'If this is so big me and Sam want equal shares as you. We'll give the boys what we think fit.'

The Kid shrugged. 'My colleague is due the major share. He's the one who's set this all up. But I'll have a word with him. Meanwhile, be ready to ride.'

'What about *my* share?' Della asked. 'There ain't gonna be much left if we split seven ways.'

The girl was still dressed in tomboy attire although she'd bought herself a new scarf and shirt. 'If these four are gonna git greedy I vote we go recruit a few guns someplace else.' She jumped to her feet. 'Come on, Kid. Seems to me they want to look a gift horse in the mouth.'

Sam hastily joined them. 'Look, we're in,' he said, earnestly. 'Just as long as we get a fair cut.'

'It's a deal, pal.' The Kid's dark eyes sparkled as he offered his hand. 'Shake on it. A Sioux never goes back on his word.'

★   ★   ★

The dark forests of the Black Hills were the domain of the yellow-eyed timber wolves which McBride could sense watching him as he rode through, and hear their lonesome howls at night. He kept his fire stacked high and although he could see their glimmering eyes they did not bother him. Bears, too, were much in evidence, but it was the time of year when they were busy filling their bellies with berries. He rode on by a female with cubs and she hardly gave him a glance. But it was tougher going than he recalled, the trail overgrown and often blocked by great cypresses brought down by the winter willawaws that screamed through the canyons from the Arctic north. It had been a hard winter.

Now mid-summer, the weather held fine, the sun firmed the ground, and grass was beginning to peep through even the rutted main street of Deadwood as he rode down through the gulch. He didn't want his horse or carbine to go missing so he liveried Satan and went looking for a lawman.

Francis Ollinger bore the title of 'Sheriff' painted on a board outside his shack, but he had a belly as big as a buffalo's hump and a backside to match which appeared to be glued to his swivel chair. He rocked back and forth, his boots up on his desk-top. He chewed on the damp butt of a cigar as he listened to what Randolph McBride had to say.

'Yep, there were two guys around called Stevens and Doyle but this is the first I've heard that they might have been cattle-thieves.'

'Would you say they were big-spenders?'

'Yep, they sure were, dropping greenbacks around like they were too hot to handle.'

'So, didn't you pull 'em in, question where it came from?'

'Mister, this town's full of riff-raff arrived from all points of the compass to try their luck at the diggings or the tables. Like you know, them that get lucky digging gen'rally lose it gambling. Do you think I got time to question every scallawag who hits town? If they don't give us no trouble then we don't bother them.'

'No,' McBride drawled, sarcastically scratching the seven days' growth of stubble on his jaw, 'it don't look like you would. You got any idea if these boys are still in town?'

'Now you mention it I ain't seen 'em around for a coupla days or more. If they're still here you'll find 'em in Number Ten.'

'You gonna help me arrest 'em, Sheriff?'

'Nope.' The sheriff tossed the cigar stub into a spittoon. 'It ain't none of my business, out of my jurisdiction, you might say. They ain't done nuthin' wrong here. You go ahead if you wanna take 'em back. Help yourself. I'm a busy man. I'm mayor of this town, and, you probably saw from the sign, I buy gold dust. Give a fair price, too.'

'You refuse to back me? What *would* make you get outa that chair?'

'Well, if it were worth my while, if there were any reward out on them boys.' He leaned over and picked up a couple of 'Wanted' posters. 'These came through the post but I clean forgot to look at 'em. Missed out on some cash there. *These* two birds were here, but they've gawn, too. Might have all gone together for all I know.'

McBride took a look at the posters. The Buckthorn Kid, 23 years, 5ft 5ins, half-breed, dark complexion, escaped convict, $500 paid for his return to the penitentiary. The other showed a picture of a buck-toothed girl, known as Della Reid, as well as other aliases. Wanted for aiding and abetting a prison escape. A reward of $200 was offered for her apprehension.

'What would happen if they committed an offence in Deadwood?' McBride demanded.

'Mister, that's a different matter.' Ollinger twiddled a last coil of hair on his balding head, finally eased himself to his feet, stretched and yawned. 'If it was a plain case of murder we would raise the Vigilante Committee an' go after 'em. But, like I said, most of us are too busy.'

'Yeah?' The big rancher, in his tall hat and loose-tied bandanna, hitched back his topcoat to adjust the heavy Remington revolver slung on his hip, and fixed the fat man with thorny eyes through narrowed lids. 'Looks like I gotta take care of things myself, don't it?'

★   ★   ★

In the narrow shebang which went by the name of No. 10, McBride downed a glass of rotgut, chased by warm beer, and asked about Sam and Joel, and their two sidekicks.

'They left town two days ago,' an old rummy croaked out. 'I saw 'em go north headin' towards Belle Fourche. They was with old Parrot Nose, the Kid, and that doxie of his who goes round in men's clothes. Looked to me like they was in a hurry.'

He bought the old-timer a bottle and went back out into the busy main street. The gulch was already in shadow from the hills hanging over it. Too late to set off now. He would have to find himself a bed for the night.

'Randy McBride! What brings you to this hell-hole? I ain't set eyes on you for ten years.'

'Alice?' He hardly recognized the woman with hennaed hair who came from the dining-room of the ramshackle joint which advertised 'Rooms'. She rushed to him and almost squashed the air out of him in her full-bodied hug. 'You've kinda rounded out, Alice.'

'Yeah, I've put on a few pounds.' She smirked up at him, her double chin trembling. 'It's the easy living. You ain't changed a bit.'

'No . . . well.' He disentangled himself with some embarrassment. 'Maybe no, maybe yes.'

'You looking for a bed? You've come to the right place. You can have the best. A double, deep duck down. You'll sleep like a babe.' She giggled up at him. 'That's if you want to sleep. I'm a respect'ble widow lady now. I got married to the funeral parlour man. He died in his sleep.'

'What did he die of?'

She beckoned him to her and whispered in his ear, 'I think I musta loved him to death' — only she didn't say loved.

McBride drew back, prudishly. 'It's just a bed I'm wanting, Alice. I'm a widow man myself, recently bereaved. I ain't here to sow my oats. I'm after some abscondees.'

'A bed is what you'll have, darlin'. But after dinner you must join me in my private parlour. We'll split a bottle and yarn about old times.'

She was comely enough, if your taste was for big ladies and, as the whiskey went down, she began to look comelier. She had been a *fille-de-joie* in her younger days, but had put away the scarlet satin for a black silk Mother Hubbard. She kept her keys on a golden sash around her waist.

It was good to talk to someone who was unrelated about his wife, and how they had met, and about his son. It was the first time he let his feelings spill out and it was as if he needed to tell someone.

'You know, I always liked you, McBride,' she said, cosying up to him as they relaxed on her horsehair sofa in the warm glow from the wood stove. 'But you didn't give a damn about me, did you?'

'I was just a youngster, getting my first taste of things. I remember you were a good teacher. But I thought you were Bill Hickok's main girl.'

'I was before he went an' married Agnes, the damn fool. She was ten years older than him, not that that matters, does it, darlin'?' she asked, tweaking his ear.

McBride moved away slightly, although her flesh was like a comfortable cushion to rest against, and what with the perfume and rustle of silk, she was beginning to make his head spin. Or was that the whiskey?

'I'll tell you straight, Alice, I ain't lookin' to get wed again.' To change the subject, he asked, 'Why do you figure

Bill sat with his back to the door that day?'

'He was inviting death. It was suicide. He was losing his sight. Decay of the optic nerve due to the clap. He couldn't see to shoot any more. He didn't want the disgrace of going down to some punk kid. So he let one shoot him in the back, instead. Personally, I think the half-wit who hit him was put up to it by some creep who'd lost at cards.'

They reminisced some more until McBride said he was going to hit the hay. 'You want me to come and tuck you up,' Alice cajoled, 'no strings attached, of course?'

'I . . . er . . . don't fancy ending up like Wild Bill,' said McBride. 'To be blunt I keep myself clean these days. Don't want to hurt your feelings, Alice, but . . . '

'I'm clean, too, hon. No need to worry about that. Come on, you know you want to.' She ushered him into his bedroom which was conveniently next door. Before he knew it she was bereft of the Mother Hubbard, her milk-white bosom spilling out from her corset as she climbed onto him, giggling with excitement. 'Anyhow,' she murmured, 'if it puts your mind at rest there are plenty of other ways I can pleasure you.' So, as he sank back into the duck down, pleasure him she did.

5

The outlaws rode out of the Black Hills back to Belle Fourche, crossed the river and headed north through western Dakota. They followed the Little Missouri for 150 miles until they reached the Badlands, a desolate wilderness studded with myriad round buttes, scored by thousands of dry creeks, or treeless streams so bitter of alkali that beast or man would have to be sore athirst to drink. There were occasional basins covered with deep sage and now and again a stream of sweet water, where their horses could forage. But mostly, even in summer, this vast tract of land was melancholy and forbidding.

Sam Stevens was glad of the leather *tapaderas* hanging from his Spanish saddle that protected his legs as, once again, they plunged down into one of innumerable deep ravines that scarred the landscape and tried to fight their way through the bottoms filled with almost impassable thickets of diamond willow and thorny buffalo berry. 'Hot dang!' he cried out, 'no wonder we gave most of this land to the damn Indians.'

In spite of his protection Sam's new four-button suit was torn, crumpled and stained, smelling, like the others, of woodsmoke from their camp-fires. Even his waxed moustache had drooped. He was not the dandy he was in Deadwood.

'Where 'n hell we going Parrot Nose?' Joel Doyle shouted, not so respectful to their leader as the Kid. 'You sure you got any idea?'

Johnson, in his derby hat and long canvas wind-shedder over his suit, pulled a small compass from his pocket. 'All I know is from the map we just keep going north. Sometime soon we oughta hit the railroad line. Look at it this way, boys, this is ideal country for a hit.'

The Kid, too, was glad of his black leather jacket and slacks, the black kid gloves that brushed off the thorns. He scorned to use a white man's saddle and rode the way he always had, bareback, with just a rawhide rope knotted twice beneath the mustang's jaw. That way he could respond to the creature's mood and movement, guiding him mainly with his knees and voice. The cruel-looking spurs were just for show, except in dire necessity.

The sky had darkened over with low, heavy cloud, and thunder rumbled ominously to the north. 'There's going to be a storm,' Della opined, as lightning flickered across the horizon. 'Ain't it time we made camp?'

She looked little different to the young cowboys, Buzz and Jim, in her battered hat, coloured shirt, jeans and boots, a gunbelt hitched around her waist. They, too, looked apprehensive. Nobody liked carrying shooting irons, or hanging on to steel-bitted bridles when lightning might strike.

'OK,' Parrot Nose agreed, swinging down. 'There's kindling aplenty in this gulch. Better git a fire going 'fore the rains come down. There's two hours of daylight left, but what the hell.'

Nor was Johnson as young as he would like to be. Three years in a penitentiary had got him out of practice for hard riding. And a hard ride it had been.

He groaned and stretched his limbs as he unsaddled his bronc. 'I'll be glad when this is over,' he confided to the Kid. 'Just this one big heist, that's all I need. You know what I'm gonna do? Retire, change my name, go to ground, and buy myself a saloon up in Virginny City someplace.'

'You know, that ain't a bad idea,' The Kid mused. 'My share's big enough maybe I'll go straight, too. I'm gittin' tired of being locked up. I've been in and out of reformatories and jailhouses since I was twelve. That's one thang the Sioux side of me cain't abide. Thass why I have to git out.'

'That's right, he's half-decent underneath,' Della put in. 'So am I. All we never had was a chance to prove it.'

'Listen to them two croakers,' Sam hooted. 'We got a right crew of milksops to rob a train with, ain't we? Two dimwitted kids, a whining 'breed, an' a thievin' bitch.'

'Shut up an' get the fire lit,' Parrot Nose growled, tossing down the body of a mountain sheep from the back of his saddle. 'We'll find out just who spills his guts when the time comes.'

He had brought down the white-rumped sheep with a lucky 'pop shot' from his shotgun. A small herd had been nibbling at cactus on a cliffside. An old ram had met his eye, gave the bleat to scoot, but one of his ewes was too late.

'That was fine shooting, Mr Johnson.' Jim Hetherington was a sallow-faced, scrawny youth, inclined to suck up to his betters. His once-white goatskin coat was soiled and straggly, tied by a thick leather belt into which a Colt Navy was

96

shoved. 'From the saddle, too!'

'That's the way you got to learn to shoot, boy, if you're coming into our profession.' The older man stroked the shotgun lovingly. It might be a three shot, but its action was fast, with traditional Scottish accuracy. 'I'm a man of instant decision. You don't have time to think twice.'

Buzz, too, a youngster of 16, was easily impressed. Malnourished since birth, his mouth was already a wreck of rotting teeth, and his nose ran constantly. 'Can I have the fur of this sheep?' he asked, stringing the carcase from a branch and slitting away the wool. 'I'll get it made into a pair of chaps.'

'Hark at him!' The Kid grinned, as he broke dead wood across his knee and fed the fire. 'Once we reach that railroad you're gonna have more to think about than duding yourself up.'

'Yeah,' Jim chimed in, 'an' with all the cash that's coming to us you can buy all the *chapareras* you want. What exactly will you expect us to do, Mr Johnson?'

Parrot Nose sat on a log, lit a cigar and surveyed them, giving a dismissive shrug. 'Maybe all you'd better do is hold the damn horses. Why don't that snotty punk wipe his nose? It ain't sightly.'

'Yeah.' The Kid grinned some more. 'Lookin' at him puts you off your grub, don't it?'

'All I'm askin' of you prairie rats,' Johnson growled, 'is to obey my orders and to be able to ride fast and shoot faster.'

'For the amount of cash you mention,' Sam said, 'I'd be glad to kill my own granny.'

'Hang on!' The Buckthorn Kid put up a hand to calm them. 'We don't want no killin' on this caper. Don't go doing anything stupid. We need to pull this off and get away clean. I ain't lookin' to be dangling from some hempen necktie.'

'Hell,' Jim yelled. 'Iffen someone

shoots at us we gotta shoot back, ain't we?'

'The Kid's right.' Johnson blew a smoke ring, studied it, and took a flask of whiskey from his side pocket. 'We don't shoot nobody 'less we're forced to. Use your brains, if you got any.' He took a sup and swallowed, put the flask back in his pocket, not offering it around. 'Chuck those sheep guts away from here, you fool. We don't want all the flies in hell buzzin' round.'

Buckthorn had cut a green holly sticky to skewer the sheep and use it as a spit on two forked sticks to roast it. 'Keep that fire blazing, boys. I'm damn hungry. I could eat the whole thing, myself.'

It took a long while to roast and was only half-cooked by the time the sky darkened and there was a crash of thunder over their heads like the sound of 10,000 drums and cymbals, making them jump instinctively and put anything iron aside as blobs of lightning fizzled about their ears.

'Shee-it!' Jim cried, trying to rig his tarpaulin poncho up over his head as the mustangs squealed their terror and tried to break free. 'This ain't good.'

'Make sure them broncs are hitched tight,' Johnson roared above the din, going to try to shelter under the ledge of a cliff himself. 'We don't want to waste three hours in the morning lookin' for 'em.'

For minutes it was as if all hell was let loose about them, the din of thunder stunning their senses, a reek of burning as a flash of lightning sheared a cottonwood and set it sizzling. But then it was over and the rain sheeted down. 'Aw, hell,' Sam moaned, as he squeezed among them disconsolately. 'This's putting the fire out.'

The Kid pulled up his collar as rain trickled down his neck and tipped from his hat brim. 'I don't care whether it's cooked or not,' he said, pulling his razor-sharp scalping knife and going over to carve himself a ragged hunk of meat. He stood and chewed. 'It ain't so bad.'

'That's all right for savages like you,' Sam remarked, as they all gathered round to join him and slice themselves greasy portions, 'but I ain't used to eatin' raw sheep.'

'It's better for you,' the Kid replied, spitting out lead pellets between mouthfuls. 'Help yourself, Della. There's plenty of it.'

Johnson produced a loaf of soggy pumpernickel bread from his bag and passed it around as they retreated to the cliff overhang. 'We might as well get what shut-eye we can, boys. It's gonna be a miserable night.'

'Well,' Joel drawled, as he wiped his mouth on his sleeve, 'I'm of the opinion you didn't ought to hog all that whiskey you got. Ain't it s'posed to be all for one and one for all?'

'You shoulda thought of bringing your own,' Johnson growled. 'I don't share my whiskey with no man. It's too precious.'

'There'll be whiskey galore once we're rich,' Jim Hetherington drooled. 'I'll be drinking it 'til it comes outa my ears.'

When the worst of the storm passed and the rain set into a steady drizzle they managed to kick some life into the fire and huddled in their waterproofs around it.

'Hell,' Sam Stevens shouted, 'if we cain't have whiskey I'm gonna have some fun with this gal. She's a reg'lar alley cat under them men's pants of her'n.' He gave a whoop and grabbed hold of Della, dragging the screaming girl away into the bushes.

The two youngsters giggled inanely, and went to urge on the fun as Della screeched and fought like a wildcat. 'Get off me,' she shouted, as she was thrown on her back and her boots and trousers dragged from her.

Suddenly a shot crashed out, the bullet nicking Sam's earlobe as it hurtled past. He turned to see the Kid standing six feet away, his Allen and Hopkins smoking. 'What 'n hell you doing?' he cried.

The Kid's teeth flashed white in the darkness, as he thumbed the hammer. 'Come on, go for it,' he dared.

'She's only a damn hoo-er. What you all fired up about? You can have her back after.' Sam glared at him. 'I'll pay you the two dollars if you want.'

'She ain't for sale.'

Della picked herself up and dressed slowly, hitching up her muddy pants and pulling on her boots, brushing herself down. 'I didn't know you cared.' Della gave the Kid a toothy smirk, and walked past him back to the fire.

'Look what you done to my ear,' Sam whined, looking at blood drops on his fingers. 'You're crazy.'

'She's my property, thassall.' Buckthorn holstered his revolver. 'I'd be obliged if you treat her with respect.'

Sam shrugged his arms at the two cowboys. 'What we got ourselves into? How'd we git mixed up with these madmen? Won't share their whiskey; won't share their wimmin,' he grumbled. 'What the hell's the matter with them?'

6

The Indian police officer, Wolf Voice, had driven his buggy in from the reservation with his two wives to the soddy school on the edge of Medora. The former Cheyenne warrior had abandoned his fringed buck-skins for the uncomfortable, high-buttoned, navy-blue uniform, his tin star of office on his chest, his gilt buttons gleaming and white gauntlets newly washed. Instead of moccasins he wore high, shiny black boots, and his black plaits hung down beneath a bowl-domed black hat.

It was mid-afternoon and the children were just running out to disperse to their various homes. Because of the distance from the reservation, their 11-year-old son, Rain-on-the-Face, had been boarding at the adjoining two-storey cabin occupied by the teacher lady, Miss Daisy Bradshaw.

'What's he been doing she wants to meet us?' he asked in his own guttural language as he climbed down and beckoned his wives to follow. The two squaws, in their shawls and long skirts, were very similar in appearance, thin-faced, dark-complexioned, and of modest mien. They were sisters. A Cheyenne preferred to have sisters as wives for they were less argumentative. 'You better come, too.'

The turves forming the walls of the school had been laid with fine exactitude so the building was a regular oblong shape, sash windows and wooden doors supplied by the federal government. Inside there were benches, a blackboard, and a desk at the front where the teacher was busy writing in a notebook with a scratchy quill pen.

'Ah, how nice of you to come, Mr Wolf Voice,' she called out. 'I'll just finish this paragraph. Take a pew all of you.'

The Cheyenne were not sure what a pew was so they hovered near the door and watched the teacher. She was a dainty little woman, dressed in a starched blouse, clasped at the throat by a cameo brooch, and rather odd baggy black culottes which she wore so she could ride astride. It was a habit frowned on by white people for some reason, but Miss Bradshaw, they had heard, was a very independent-spirited lady.

How many summers the teacher had seen was difficult to judge, too. She had the odd look of white women, a little upturned nose, dimpled cheeks, green eyes, pink and white skin and a pointed chin. Her thick brown hair was scooped up into a bun like a loaf on the top of her head, held by a comb, wispy strands floating free. She had a shrill, precise way of speaking, and her head, it was said, contained much useless knowledge. How could it all float around in there?

Wolf Voice and his wives were distracted by the arrival of Rain-in-the-Face, dark-faced and dark-haired like them, but a handsome boy. His father caught him by the scruff of his neck. 'You been fighting? What you done? Have you brought disgrace on us?'

'*Heyah!*' Miss Bradshaw called out, for she had fair knowledge of the Siouan language and was attempting to write a dictionary of it in her spare time. '*Hunkaschila hecheto welo.*' In English that would mean, 'The young man has done very well'.

Daisy Bradshaw quickly blotted her entry and closed the notebook, laying the pen aside and smiling as she rose. 'Who is the boy's mother? I can never remember which of you is which?'

'Me?' High Moon said, proud but solemn. 'Why have you brought us here?'

'I want to talk to you about Rain-in-the-Face. He has been attending here for three years now and he has made amazing progress. He is a very bright boy.' She tried to translate her words for the benefit of the women. She patted the boy's fringed head. 'You had better run out and play while we talk about this.'

When he had gone she said, 'Frankly, I think your son is wasting his talents here. He could have a great future. I want you to let me send him to a church school in St Louis where he will have an excellent education until he is sixteen. After that, who knows, he could be a lawyer or journalist. He might even become a judge, or run for Congress. It is not unknown.'

Wolf Voice and his wife looked stunned until High Moon cried, 'No, he is our son. You have taken our land, but you are not taking our son away from us.'

'But don't you see? He could go on to university, maybe Princeton. He could speak out for you, try to insure that you are not treatied out of what's left of your land, as you were before.'

'You mean,' Wolf Voice said, 'he would be taken away and we would not see him again?'

'No, I would be glad to go with him

on the railroad to Bismarck and catch a paddle steamer down to St Louis. I would enrol him in the presbyterian college. It is a charity. There would be no charge. He could, of course, come home to see you in the holidays.'

'He would no longer be our son,' High Moon replied, glumly. 'No, this is not good.'

'What else is there for him? To stay on that bleak reservation all his life? To become an Indian policeman at eleven dollars a month?'

As a teacher Daisy Bradshaw did not earn a great deal more herself. She stroked a strand of hair from her eyes and smiled at them. 'I want you to think seriously about this. It is the boy's, your people's future. It is up to you.'

'Hey, look what I've found,' Rain-in-the-Face shouted, running in. He had a dead porcupine in his hands, and dropped it on the floor. 'Somebody shot it.'

'Take that away,' his mother scolded.

'It is full of fleas.'

Daisy Bradshaw examined it with interest. 'A genus of quadruped of the rodent or gnawing order. It has a distinct family, the hystricidae. They are found in several parts of the world. See, child, the two incisors that grow throughout its lifetime. He must be quite old. His hair turns into quills. You use them, of course, for your breast plates or as decoration. See the reverse barbs on the ends? They can choke a wolf or a dog that attacks them. I think I'll pull a couple out. I can use them as pen holders. Careful now.'

'We know what this creature is,' High Moon cried, angrily. 'We do not need you to tell us. We call him the spiky apple-eater. He eats the bark of trees, too. One raided our corn.'

Wolf Voice silenced her. Tall, broad and strong-jawed, he had once been a renowned warrior. As a dog soldier his task had been to police his Cheyenne camp, restrain any over-eager braves, intervene in quarrels. So he took easily to being a white man's officer, along with his battalion of brother Cheyenne, and obeyed orders implicitly.

'You must not insult the white teacher lady,' he advised in his own language. 'She wants what she thinks is good for our son. She has much knowledge. We must talk about this.'

High Moon sighed and backed away to stand beside her silent sister. What could she do? It was as if a great gulf was already separating her from the boy. He was chattering to the teacher lady in the strange words as if she was the one he liked to be with. She could not fight the white teacher and her knowledge.

She could not fight them all.

'Well,' Daisy said brightly, 'I hope you will, at least, all stay for supper before you go.'

★ ★ ★

When Parrot Nose Johnson and his would-be train robbers hit the Northern Pacific Railroad they turned west

111

and headed along the single track towards the small township of Medora. In places the route had been blasted through solid rock and Buckthorn kept a sharp look-out for a suitable spot to set their ambush. 'Look at that sheer cliff wall,' he sang out. 'Y'could jump on the roof of the train easy from there. It'll have slowed on the upgrade. What's your plan, chief?'

'I ain't sure yet,' Parrot Nose replied. 'Maybe we can hit it when it pulls into Medora.'

'You ain't sure?' Sam Stevens hollered. 'Ain't it time you were dang sure? It's gonna be along any time soon.'

'Mind your own damn business.' Johnson swivelled his mustang around to face him. 'I've told you prairie trash your job's to obey orders. The Kid and me are taking a look at the lie of the land.'

Joel spat a gob of baccy juice towards the portly gent in his derby and, when Johnson moved on, growled, 'We gonna let him talk to us like that?'

'Sure as hell we ain't,' Sam replied, eyeing the two scruffy youngsters, 'but we gotta play along with him for a while. You boys remember who's side you're on and be ready to go for your guns when I give the nod.'

The boy, Jim, bared his ruined teeth and hissed, 'We're with you, Sam. You're the boss. Not him.'

They ambled on for another twenty miles until the township of Medora came into view. It had been founded and named by the Marquis de Mores after his bride, Medora von Hoffman, daughter of a rich New York banker. They lived in amazing style in a twenty-six room chateau he had had built along the Little Missouri River, with servants to cater for their every whim. They owned sheep and cattle ranches, and a stage line, and regarded the North Dakota Badlands as their own. There was wealth aplenty in these parts for the lucky few.

The first building the outlaws saw on the edge of town was the soddy school with its adjoining two-storey wooden house. 'Hey, look at that purty gal,' Sam Stevens cried, spotting Daisy Bradshaw sweeping the steps of her porch. 'Let's go have a chat.'

'Listen, you half-wits,' Parrot Nose thundered, 'I don't want you doing nuthin' in this town while we're here to draw attention to us. Just damn well behave yourselves if you want to work for me.'

'Aw, we only gonna pass the time of day,' Sam called out, as he spurred his bronc towards the schoolhouse.

The others followed, trotting after him, as Sam doffed his hat and pulled in his mustang beside the porch. 'Howdy, Ma'am. Or is you a miss, might I ask?'

'My name's Miss Bradshaw.' She rested a hand on her hip and eyed him, severely. 'I run the school here. How can I help you?'

Buzz pulled in his mustang and sniggered. 'I can think of plenty ways she kin help us, eh, Sam? What kinda

114

damn trousers she wearin'? Why ain't she wearin' a skirt?'

'Maybe she's a loose-livin' hoo-er, like Della here?' Buzz chortled. 'Maybe she could give us all some of her time?'

'You *what?*' Miss Bradshaw rested her hands on the broom and stared at them, haughtily. 'Did I hear right? Who the hell do you think you're talkin' to?'

'We're talkin' to you, honey.' Sam vaulted from his horse to land on the wooden veranda and tried to grab hold of Daisy. 'You might be a bit long in the tooth, but you good enough for me. How much you charge, hon? I'll give ya three dollars for a quickie upstairs. I bet that's as much as you earn in a day.'

'How *dare* you?' Daisy evaded his clutches and swung the broom, catching Sam a thwack across the head and dislodging his hat. 'Get out of here before I — '

Sam twisted the broom from her hands and dived in to grab her in a bearhug as Daisy screamed and kicked. He tossed her over his shoulder and headed towards the door. 'She's gonna git a good stiff talkin' to, thass what she's going to git.'

An explosion shattered the Sunday quiet as Parrot Nose Johnson pulled his new-fangled German Mauser automatic and a slug plummeted into the woodwork of the doorpost, nearly taking off Sam's other ear. 'Put that woman down, you stupid son-of-a-bitch.'

Sam froze then slowly let Miss Bradshaw slide to the floor. She struggled free of him and gave him a resounding slap across the face. He stared at her, holding his burning cheek. 'I'll remember that, lady,' he snarled.

'Get back on your bronc, you sawdust-brained string of piss,' Johnson shouted, as the Kid gave a loud, caustic laugh. 'Didn't you hear me say we didn't want no trouble in this town?'

Sam scooped up his hat sullenly and jumped back on his horse as Johnson raised his derby to Daisy. 'I must apologize to you, miss. I'm a gov'ment surveyor and these scum are the best I could get to accompany me on my travels. I do hope you won't take this any further.'

Daisy straightened her blouse and hitched up her culottes, taking a look at the seven motley riders. 'If it's a whore you're looking for you've come to the wrong place. Might I remind you, sir, that in these parts men better than these have ended hanging from a telegraph pole for molesting, nay merely *insulting* a decent woman. So, think yourselves lucky I am not vindictive and be on your way.'

'My profuse apologies once more, miss. No harm done.' Parrot Nose Johnson opened his check suit and consulted a gold watch as big as an onion on its chain. 'Before we go might I check the date? My timepiece tells me it's July the 30th. Would that be correct?'

'Yes,' she replied, coolly. 'That's right.'

'So the express from Chicago would be due through tomorrow, the 31st?'

'True. Why?'

'We wish to embark, that's all. At what time exactly is it due here?'

'It's generally here on the dot of four o'clock every Monday and Thursday at this time of year.'

'Thank you, Miss,' Parrot Nose said. 'That's as I hoped. Good day to you. One other question, who's the big cheese, as you might say, in this place? Do you have a lawman?'

'No. The big cheese, in your words, is the Marquis de Mores. He owns this town and runs it in a very orderly fashion. He is the law. I would advise you to warn your 'scum', as you call them, not to step on his toes. He is a man of very unstable temper. Goodbye to you.' As they rode away she called out, 'I might say I agree with your epithets. Ill-mannered skunks indeed.'

Sam waved his arm, dismissively. 'Ar, git lost, sister. Ye're too skinny fer my taste, anyhow.'

★ ★ ★

A smell of death offended Buckthorn's keen, half-Sioux nostrils as they rode into Medora. A strong smell of blood. It emanated from a vast slaughter-house built alongside the river, the biggest and most modern in the West. Why go to the trouble of herding live sheep and cattle into the railroad trucks? reasoned the Marquis de Mores. Wouldn't it be more economical to slaughter them on the spot and transport their carcasses in refrigerated cars on the new Northern Pacific line, either to Chicago or to New York? Well, *he* thought it would be and spent a good slice of his wife's fortune, some $250,000 on the huge plant and in forming a refrigerator-car company with ice plants at twelve points along the railroad.

Whether the energetic Frenchman's latest scheme would pay off was yet to be seen. Other of his business schemes had turned out to have fatal flaws. His stage line from Medora to Deadwood, for instance, had failed not just due to lack of custom but because he lost a vital mail contract. Nonetheless the Marquis Antoine Amedée Marie Vincent Mance de Valambrosa de Mores, to give him his full name, was unabashed. He had opened a string of stores in New York city to sell beef, mutton and lamb straight from his slaughterhouse.

So, when Parrot Nose Johnson, and his odd assortment of followers, rode into Medora they found the place buzzing like a beehive. A river of woolly sheep from de Mores' own ranch was at that moment being herded along the main street towards the meat packing plant.

'What in tarnation's that?' Sam Stevens hooted, as they saw standing outside the town's Alhambra Hotel a cumbersome, gilt-enscrolled coach with a team of not four but eight grey horses. He rode up and took a peek inside the window. 'There's a goddamn bed and table in here,' he yelled, 'and, hail, its got its own bar. Jest look at that silverware!'

He was prodded on the shoulder by a rifle barrel wielded by a bellicose guard sat beside the driver, who told him in no uncertain terms to clear off. 'We don't want no ruffians here.'

'Who 'n hail you think you're talking to?' Sam's hand went instinctively to the pearl butt of his S & W, but Parrot Nose restrained him.

'Yeah, you boys look the worse for wear,' he muttered. 'You better go have some fun in some brass knuckle dive. I'm booking in here. Don't forget what I told ya, keep ya noses clean.'

Johnson climbed down, painfully, from his horse, tossed the reins to a boy to lead it around to the stables in the back and clambered up the steps to the hotel. He banged the bell at the desk and booked in a room. There he washed, shaved and tidied himself, scraped the mud from his check suit, plastered his thinning hair neatly across his scalp, and clattered back down to the dining-room and lounge bar.

At a table in the centre of the room sat a tall, fierce-looking man, his moustaches waxed to pinpoints, attired in a high-collared military uniform of some foreign scarlet and black design, stripes down the sides of his pants and shiny boots. His curly black hair was primped and brilliantined and he was talking animatedly to a burly, short-sighted young man in a more conventional hunter's outfit.

Beside them sat a haughty young woman, her dark hair drawn back severely, parted centrewise, in a dress of purple taffeta clasped at the throat by a gold chain from which dangled a gem that immediately caught Parrot Nose's attention.

'Would that be this mark-ee I bin hearin' about?' he low-voiced to some sort of be-suited business man who was at an adjoining table. 'Mind if I jine ya?'

'Yes,' the gent agreed, nodding primly. 'That is the marquis and his lady wife, Medora. Quite beautiful, isn't she?'

'She sure is a bobby dazzler. So's that jewel dangling under her chin. Big as a chicken egg, ain't it? Lovely cut to it. Y' can see the flash of it from here.'

He stuffed a napkin into his waistcoat and studied the menu, keeping an ear wagging to catch what Mores was on about. Apparently he was trying to interest the other dude into shipping salmon from the Columbia River to New York.

'By Godfrey! That sounds a little tricky,' the chubby chap replied, peering through his spectacles. 'I fear we might get out of our *depth* there.' He roared with laughter. 'Get it?'

'You ain't kiddin', buster,' Parrot Nose opined, winking at his neighbour. 'Sounds like a real crack-brained idea.'

The bald-headed diner, in a church suit, collar and cravat, touched his lips with a finger and waggled his head, disapprovingly. He leaned forward and stage-whispered, 'Careful what you say, sir. The marquis has a very fiery temper. He once killed a grizzly with just his knife.'

'You don't say? Who's the other dude.'

'Mr Theodore Roosevelt. He has a ranch in the Badlands, too. I wouldn't underestimate him, either. A young man of very sturdy constitution. I've seen him fell a rude, rough wrangler who harassed him with one blow.'

'Yeah? How about the good-looker? Is she a superwoman, too.'

'Well, she rides magnificently and is a crack shot. I've heard she can pick off prairie chickens from the saddle.' The gent lowered his eyes and attended to his food when de Mores glowered across, his dark eyes flashing beneath heavy brows. 'It's best not to say any more. I run the bank here,' he whispered, 'and depend on these gentlemen's custom.'

'The bank, huh?' Parrot Nose grinned, met the marquis's monocled eye and tipped a finger to his brow in salute.

'I never thought this town would turn out to be so interesting.'

'So, what do you do, sir? What brings you here?'

'I'm a gov'ment surveyor.' Johnson's bright idea of an alibi had been suggested by a marked plinth they had passed on the trail. 'You probably know that near here is the geographical centre of the USA. Well, we been havin' our doubts. I'm here to check it out.'

7

'Whoo-oooh!' The steam whistle of the big locomotive echoed through the canyons as the Buckthorn Kid and Slippery Sam Stevens crouched among sage bushes on the edge of a twenty-foot sheer cliff. 'Here it comes,' the Kid yelled. 'You ready?'

'Ready as I'll ever be,' Sam replied, watching the column of smoke pouring into the sky and listening to the rasping, huffing engine as it laboured up the incline, getting nearer and nearer. 'Ready to blast this baby to hell and back.'

The outlaws had cantered out of Medora early that morning following the single track east for twenty miles or so until they found the suitable ambush site. Parrot Nose, Joel Doyle, Della and the two youngsters were now waiting with the horses a couple of miles back up the track.

'It all depends on us if we're gonna stop this damn train,' the Kid shouted. 'You go first. Make sure you jump well forward on the van. You don't wanna go rolling off the end.'

'Sure, I know what to do.' But Sam was tense, his fists clutched tight. Even though it was slowed by the slight incline it looked to be going at a pretty fast speed. 'You make sure you don't drop that crowbar, 'breed.'

Inside the Wells Fargo armoured baggage van two guards, Morgan O'Malley and Seth Adams, were playing cards with the conductor, Joe Wood. They were plain clothes investigators and being two of the company's best men, they had been brought in to guard the large sum of cash being transported, $10,000 in greenbacks for the Marquis ·de Mores, and another $30,000 destined to be exchanged for gold dust at Virginia City, north Montana.

'We'll be in Medora in half an hour,' Seth said, glancing at his watch. 'How about I go get a bite to eat? I'm starving. It's four on the dot.'

'Right,' Morgan muttered, more interested in his hand. 'When we reach town jump down and take a good look around.'

'Why?' the elderly conductor, in his company uniform, hollered. 'You expecting trouble?'

'You never know,' Morgan said. 'Let him out, Joe.'

The conductor found his keys and unlocked the heavy iron-clad door, seeing Seth out and locking up again.

The detective, in his suit and homburg hat, glanced up at the sheer low walls of cliff passing by on either side. The rain had ceased and the sun was shining in a blue North Dakota sky. He stepped across the open gap to the Pullman private compartments, walking along the corridor until he reached the restaurant car and its steaming kitchen. He found himself a seat at the far end of the crowded compartment and beckoned to a black steward to order.

Beyond the restaurant car were two carriages for what you might call hoi polloi, and beyond them two more goods vans or general luggage, then the big locomotive with its cow-catcher grille and its tall stack belching smoke back at them.

On the cliff the smoke billowed around the Kid and Sam as the iron horse rattled past beneath them. 'Right, now!' The young rustler appeared to hesitate nervously, so Buckthorn gave his elbow a push. 'Go!'

He watched Sam leap down and land safely on the roof of the goods van behind the engine, hold himself steady, then leap forward onto the tender of sawn logs, his S & W in hand. His job was to hold the gun on the engineer and stoker and to stop the train at the appointed spot.

But the Kid had no time to follow his progress. He was peering down through the clouds of acrid smoke at the coaches passing below him. 'Here it comes,' he muttered, seeing the armoured car. He gripped the iron 'jemmy' in one hand, pitched himself into space, landing lightly in his moccasins on the roof of the car.

'What was that?' Inside the armoured car the Wells Fargo man had heard a light thump on the roof. He looked upwards, drawing his revolver from a holster on his belt.

'What?' Joe asked. 'I didn't hear nuthin'. You're gittin' edgy, Morgan. You imagined it.'

Parrot Nose had figured out that the armoured vehicle had one flaw, the small, square skylight. It was made of specially strengthened glass, but no glass had yet been invented that couldn't be broken.

The Kid examined it as he knelt on the swaying roof, put the crowbar to the curved lip of the edge of the skylight and tried to prise it off, gritting his teeth and using all his strength. No, that was no good. It would have to be the glass. He began hacking at it with the point of the iron bar.

'I ain't imagining that!' Morgan

O'Malley jumped to his feet and stared up at the skylight. He could see the shadowy shape of fists holding a heavy implement pounding at it. 'There's somebody trying to force his way in. Well, I'll be damned!'

'He won't git far,' Joe Wood cried, finding his shotgun. 'We'll be in Medora 'fore he gits through that glass. It's three inches thick, real solid.'

'Yeah, you think so?'

'If he does he's gonna git a real hot reception, whoever he is.'

Morgan cursed and sighed. 'It's a damn shame we ain't got some way of contacting Seth. He could get back and pick him off. He'd be a sitting duck.'

'Well, we ain't, but once we get into Medora they'll spot him. Jest listen to him hammering.'

'I can't help but listen, can I? First we got to get to Medora. That might not be what he's planning.'

Up along in the cab of the locomotive Sam Stevens was grinning at the success he was having, toting his Smith

& Wesson self-cocker and holding it to the head of the begoggled driver as his grimy-faced fireman backed away out of the line of fire. He peered out of the cab and glimpsed up in front, horsemen on the line as they left the cliff ravine. 'There they are,' he shouted. 'Get ready to slam on your anchors and bring this baby to a halt or I'll be bringing your life to a halt. Believe me, I ain't kidding. You two give me no trouble you'll be OK.'

'All right, mister, no need to jab me with that thing.' The engineer slowly applied the brake handle. 'I'm slowing down now nice and easy.'

'Good for you, boys. This gun's got a hair trigger so we don't want no jolting.'

Sparks flew as the wheels clamped and screeched along the iron rails and the great locomotive slid past the waiting horsemen. 'Howdy, boys,' Sam shouted. 'Nice to see ya. How's that for timing?'

Parrot Nose pulled his bandanna up over his face. It muffled his voice slightly as he shouted, gruffly, 'Git them two outa the cab. Buzz, you keep 'em covered. Jim, you make sure you hang on to them hosses.'

He started to ride up the track alongside the train, his three-barrel shotgun raised in his right hand. 'Joel, follow me,' he called, 'and keep an eye out in case any of these passengers try to play hero.'

'What's going on?' a man shouted, leaning from a window and chomping on a cigar.

'You'll find out,' Joel growled as he passed by.

Sam left the railroad men to Buzz who, with his carbine, beckoned them to step to the side of the track. 'Don't take your eyes of 'em, boy,' he instructed.

'I'll hold 'em 'til hell freezes over,' Buzz shouted, ecstatically. 'Or 'til I'm told otherwise.'

'Come with me, Della. We'll see what stray dollars we can shake out in here,' Sam called, passing the goods vans and climbing up into the first carriage. 'You go in the far door and cover me. Some of these fat chickens look ripe for roasting.'

A good many of the passengers were tourists arriving in high summer to travel on from Miles City to take a look at the world's first national park, the Yellowstone basin established twelve years before, with its wondrous hot springs and shooting geysers. Women screamed and hugged children to them as Sam appeared in the doorway and fired off a shot which whistled past their heads and embedded itself in the ceiling.

'All right, folks, just keep your places and you won't git hurt,' he shouted. 'If any of you *hombres* is carrying iron I'd advise you to take 'em out real slow and toss 'em through the windows. Otherwise there could be trouble.'

'Yes, there sure could,' Della yelled, from the far end, unable to control her excitement and firing off another shot that hit the ceiling but ricocheted, ripping a feathered hat from a woman's head before smashing a window as it exited. She, too, had her bandanna over her face, and swaggered forward a few paces. 'I'd advise you to git out your wallets, jewellery and valuables ready to toss into the gunnysack my playmate'll be bringing along.'

Several of the men stood reluctantly and removed revolvers from their belts, throwing them through the open windows. 'You won't get away with this,' one of them warned.

'Oh, no? Just you watch us,' Sam said, scorning to hide his face behind a mask. 'Thank you, gents, that's the sensible thing to do. Now, if you'd just oblige with your wallets. Don't try keeping anything back. That kinda trick might make me turn real nasty.'

He moved along the central aisle, waving the revolver threateningly under folks' noses, grinning at awed children. 'Yes, son, I'm the new Jesse James. Come on, lady, give me that ring.'

The woman began protesting that it

was her wedding ring, but Sam reached forward and twisted it from her. 'Get on your feet, you old haybag. What, you ain't got nuthin'? Who you kidding? Pull up your damn skirts. Let's see what you got.'

'I'm a widow,' the large lady cried, bursting into tears. 'Please don't leave me destitute.'

'Pull your skirt up. Higher! Good,' Sam screamed, his face contorted with wrath. 'Now let's take a look in your drawers. Jeez, what a horrible sight. It'll put me off sex for years. But, just as I thought!' He clutched hold of a pouch of coins and yanked it from her, dropping it in his sack. 'Try to cheat me, would you?' He smashed her in the face with the back of his fist and she collapsed back on her seat.

'OK,' Sam yelled. 'Don't anybody else try any tricks like that. Come on, I'll have that watch, mister, and that stickpin. Hurry it up, I'm losing my patience.'

'All right,' Della cried, 'you've got

enough here. Let's move on. We ain't got much time. It's in the Pullmans there'll be the real pickings. We're not interested in nickels and dimes.'

'True,' Sam agreed, with a smile. 'Just stay in your seats, folks, and you'll soon be on your way. I'd like to thank you for your contributions. So long all.'

He followed Della on into the next compartment, insisting they pause and frisk every person who looked promising. When they reached the restaurant car he bumped into a black waiter with a silver tray over his head. 'Get outa my way,' Sam shouted, pushing him in the face sending tray and pots clattering.

Seth Adams had kept his seat when the train was brought to a halt, peering from the window to see what was going on. He watched two armed men in masks go cantering their mustangs along to the armoured car. He was in two minds what to do. He doubted they would have much luck breaking into the armoured car. Might it not be best to lie doggo for a bit and try to take out their armed colleagues rather than risk a bullet in the back?

But Seth Adams panicked as he heard Sam and Della clomping along through the second car and yelling at folks to hand over their goodies. He decided to make a move back towards the armoured van. He heard a crash of silver as Sam collided with the waiter and was almost to the door to the kitchens when he heard a voice call out, 'Hey, mister, where do you think you're off to?'

Adams turned and saw the young outlaw, in his muddy four-button suit, aiming a Smith & Wesson at him. He was a good sixty feet away. A difficult shot in a crowded carriage. Seth forced a smile. For all the young punk knew he might be just a businessman. 'I gotta go to the john,' he shouted. 'I been taken short. Here, you can have my wallet.'

'Ah, poor booby, did we frighten you?' But the smile froze on Sam's face when instead of a wallet the guy produced a Colt Peacemaker and pumped out a shot. His expression changed to one of surprised agony as the bullet hit him in the chest like a sack of bricks, knocking him back against the restaurant car door. 'I'm hit,' he choked out. 'You bastard! What did you do that for?'

For answer the detective crouched forward, gripping the revolver in two hands and cracked out two more slugs to thud into Sam's chest. The young outlaw screamed out and slowly slid down to leave blood streaks on the door as he expired, falling over in a foetal position.

Adams stared at him, then turned to go on his way. 'How about me, mister?' a more shrill voice rang out.

The detective turned to see what appeared to be an avenging youth, masked, in jeans, check shirt, and Stetson pulled low over his eyes. But, as he went to fire, Della's bullet got to him first by a micro-second, toppling him back onto a kicking, hysterical lady. 'Get off me,' she screamed.

Della ducked as she fired and the detective's bullet thudded over her head into the woodwork of the door. She strode forward and, as Adams tried to right himself, pulling himself up over the terrified woman, the girl sent another slug flying to smash into the back of his head. The woman, splattered with blood, bone and brains, went into a fit of hysteria as Adams slumped upon her.

'Let that be a lesson to y'all,' Della snarled, going back to take a look at the dead Sam and snatching the S & W and the sack from his fists. 'Now y'all jest hurry it up and git your cash out, 'cause I ain't in no arguing mood. One's dead, so two won't matter to me.'

Along at the armoured car Parrot Nose, Joel and the Kid weren't having a lot of luck. The conductor, Joe Wood, had refused to open up in spite of threats shouted through the door to him. The Kid was still hammering away at the skylight but to little effect. 'This glass is like rubber. The iron just bounces off it. Hot damn, you got that dynamite, Mr Johnson? That's the only way we're gonna git in this thang.'

'Fer Christ's sake, don't tell 'em who I am, you idiot. Yeah, I've got it. Where you want it? Up there?'

'Yeah, I'll blow this damn window to smithereens. You hear me in there. You've one last chance to surrender and throw out your guns.'

Joe glanced at Morgan as they heard the muffled words. 'What'll we do? They mean business.'

Morgan licked his lips, retreating. 'Get back in the corner behind the safe. That should protect us. Be ready to fire.'

'OK, they've asked for it,' the Kid yelled, getting mad. 'Toss me up two sticks and a bit of rock. That should do it.'

'Don't overdo it,' Parrot Nose warned, but took the dynamite from his saddle-bag and went to throw it, but paused. 'Make sure you catch this. Don't play butterfingers.'

'Come on,' the Kid urged, deftly catching the sticks and then the rock, which he used to hold them in place over the window. He pulled a small, silver vesta case from his pocket and struck a match, igniting the fuses.

'Git them mustangs back a bit, boys,' he grinned as the fuses fizzled. 'This might make a mess.'

'Whoomph!' Buckthorn leaped from the van roof to land in the bushes below, a second before the dynamite exploded, rocking the van on its wheels and ripping a jagged hole in the roof.

Showered with bits of wood, iron and dust, Parrot Nose and Joel tried to control their horses as they whinnied and whirled away. The Kid pulled out his Allen and Hopkins nickel-plated revolver and hoisted himself back up to the top of the van. He cocked the pistol and fired a wild, warning shot down through the smoking hole.

'You still gonna argue?' he yelled, and, when there was no reply, peered cautiously in.

Morgan and Joe were trying to get to their feet, their heads reeling, their eardrums bleeding, their clothes mostly tattered and half-torn from their bodies, their faces blackened. They raised their arms and tottered forward, all fight forgotten.

The Kid leapt down lightly to join them. 'Why 'n hell you have to argue for? You ain't gonna get no medals. Just gimme the keys.'

'You win,' Joe muttered, hardly able to hear his own voice and walked unsteadily across to unlock the main door to let Johnson and Doyle climb in.

'Now the keys for the safe,' the Kid said. 'Open up.'

'We can't,' Morgan protested. 'Only the Wells Fargo manager in Medora knows the combination.'

'Shee-it!' Johnson gave a whistle of irritation. 'You boys certainly try to complicate things.' He passed his saddle-bags to Buckthorn. 'There's some more explosive. Get to work, Kid. Try not to send us all to Kingdom

Come, if you please.'

'Doncha worry, Mr er — if you'd all care to wait outside.' He took a bag of gunpowder from the leather bags and tried to poke it into the keyholes and hinges of the big, solid safe. Then he stuffed two dynamite sticks in the inch-space beneath it. He carefully lit the fuses. 'Hell,' he said, with a reckless grin, jumping up to sit cross-legged on top of the safe. 'I'll stay for the ride.'

The explosion blew the door from the van's hinges, but because he was so close to it Buckthorn rode out the blast without injury. He looked down to see the safe door had swung open. He jumped down and peered inside. 'Jeez,' he whispered, picking out a wad of brand new fifty-dollar notes. 'I ain't never seed so much spondulix.'

Meanwhile Della was busy reaping rewards from the passengers in the elegant Pullman sitting-rooms. A lady screamed as the girl in boy's clothing pushed inside, waggling a gun under nose. 'Right, you rich bitch. Now you gonna learn to give to the needy.' She ripped from her neck a gold and ruby necklace. 'I'll have this for a start.'

Suddenly an explosion crashed out. 'Christ! What was that? I'd better go see what's going on. Sounds like the Kid's been up to his tricks.'

What she found was Johnson, Joel and Buckthorn busy stuffing wads of dollar bills into saddle-bags. 'We've hit the jackpot!' the Kid yelled, excitedly. 'Stick some of these in your shirt, Della.'

The buck-toothed girl gawped as he handed her two wads. 'How much is there?'

'If my information is correct, as it seems to be,' Johnson said, 'there must be forty thousand dollars here. Hot dang, Kid, we've done it. I knew we would. This is the big one I've been waiting for all my life.'

'It won't do you no good,' the conductor whined, poking his blackened face through the door. 'All the numbers of those notes are sequential.

They'll soon track them down.'

'Ah, shut up,' Johnson replied, 'you're only jealous. Here,' he tossed four fifties to him. 'Thanks for your help.'

Joe Wood looked around, guiltily, to make sure Morgan wasn't watching, but he had gone to sit in the weeds. He quickly slid the notes into his pocket. 'Why not? I need some compensation for my ringing head.'

The train passengers watched dumbfounded for the outlaws had begun whooping with glee as the news was broken to them, and started hugging each other and dancing around.

'Where's Sam?' Joel asked.

'He's day-ed,' Della drawled.

'What? Who killed him?'

'Some Wells Fargo man. See, I got his card. Don't worry, I took him out. It was a fair fight.'

Buzz, Jim, Joel and Johnson fell silent, staring at her, and the Kid exploded, 'Jeesis Christ, Della! You mean you killed him?'

'Sure.' She shrugged and smiled. 'I

beat him to the draw. Nobody messes with me. Sam weren't so lucky.'

'Are you crazy?' the Kid howled. 'You know what this means, girl? They'll make you kick air. They'll hang you outa hand. And us, too.'

'They gotta catch us, first.' She grinned again, swinging onto her mustang. 'Come on, what's the matter with y'all.' She hitched the gunnysack of baubles to her saddle horn. 'Let's git.'

Joe and Morgan dived for cover as the gang of desperadoes began hollering again, riding their horses back and forth, hoorahing the passengers, shooting over their heads, making them dive back from the windows. Then they watched as the robbers crossed the rail and galloped off in an easterly direction until they disappeared into the maze of the Badlands ravines.

8

Medora was practically deserted when McBride rode in on his stallion, the long, wooden meat-packing station silent apart from the moaning of cattle crammed into adjoining corrals to await their fate. There was a sprinkling of women gossiping, and children playing, watching him go by, and a few old-timers on the sidewalks, but the saloons were deserted and of men in their prime there were none.

He had followed the winding, 250-mile long former coach trail from Deadwood rather than go across country due north, keeping Satan plodding on at a steady lope, getting what rest he could at nights, but away again before dawn. He had hoped to cut down the two-day lead the cattle thieves had on him, but it looked as if he might be too late.

McBride rode on through the main street and skirted the cluster of pitch-roofed cabins until he came to a soddy school house, with its bell tower, on the edge of town. Smoke was rising from the chimney of a wooden cottage and a young woman was in a garden behind a white-painted picket fence hanging out her smalls.

'Howdy,' the rancher called, reining in and touching his hatbrim. 'Where is everybody?'

'They've gone,' she replied, eyeing the tall, dusty stranger severely, not knowing who he might be. 'Most of the men. Didn't you hear about the robbery?'

'What robbery?'

'The express train held up outside of town. Two men killed. A dreadful business. They got away with forty thousand dollars, would you believe? The marquis drummed all able-bodied men into a posse. He's gone after them. Surely somebody at the Wells Fargo office will tell you about it, if you're interested?'

'It's locked,' McBride said. 'This is bad news, but not unexpected to me. I had an idea them young ne'er-do-wells might get gun crazy.'

'You know them?' She paused in the act of hanging a pair of damp frilled bloomers to the line, taking a peg from her teeth. 'How's that?'

Maybe, it crossed her mind, he was one of them. Maybe she should get back inside the house and lock the door? Sitting the powerful, snorting horse, a carbine slung across his back, his jowls unshaven, a big bandanna hanging around his neck, and his wide-brimmed hat pulled low over his brow, the man did have the air of some desperado.

'I got a purty good idea who they are. I been followin' 'em for five hundred miles. They stole some cattle from a neighbour of mine. I'm looking for a reckoning.' McBride sniffed the air; an appetizing aroma was drifting from the kitchen of the cottage. 'Know any place I can get a half-decent meal in town?'

'Who are you, might I ask? Some sort of manhunter?'

'Nope. Randolph McBride, rancher along Pumpkin Creek, Montana.' He removed his hat and pushed back with his fingers his thick, wavy hair from his suntanned brow. His grey eyes in their slits suddenly seemed to clash and set sparks to hers, which were deep green as jewels and glinted in the dying sun. 'You,' he said, 'I take it, are the school-marm?'

'That's true.' She held his gaze, deciding that his face did not have criminal configurations, and, indeed, if somewhat gaunt, was handsome and pleasing. She began to walk back with her empty wash basket to her open door and McBride noted that her figure was lithe and lissom beneath the culottes and starched white blouse. In fact, she was a real neat little body and he felt forlorn to see her go. But she turned and said, with a smile, 'I wonder if you would call my cooking half-decent? We've a meal ready on the stove if you'd care to join us.'

'I'd be glad to give you my opinion,' he replied, with a ready grin, wondering who 'we' might be. Maybe she was married? 'Shall I put my hoss in your stable?'

'Of course. You can wash up round the back. I'll find you a towel.'

The 'we' turned out to be an Indian boy named Rain-in-the-Face, who asked a few pertinent questions over the meal, mainly about his horse. 'He's huge. Is he a stallion?'

'Sure is,' Randolph said, as he wolfed down a plate of stew. 'Eighteen hands. Biggest there is.'

'Where did you get him from?'

'He was my wife's.' The sudden memory of Rose cut into him like a knife wound and he paused, forced to put his hand to his brow for a few moments to collect himself. 'I'm sorry,' he said. 'This ain't manly. She ain't been dead long. The horse killed her. It was an accident.'

'There is nothing unmanly, Mr

McBride, about having deep feelings for a loved one. I'm sorry to hear of your misfortune. You were hungry.' She rose to clear the plates to spare his embarrassment. 'Can I tempt you with some blueberry pie?'

'Yeah!' McBride patted his belly to change the subject. 'That Mulligan stew was the bee's knees. But I still got a bit of room down there. This is real friendly of you, Miss Bradshaw.'

'I'm sure you'd do the same for me if I were passing by. It's Western hospitality, isn't it? Call me Daisy. It's less formal. But,' she added sharply, as an afterthought, 'please don't get any other ideas.'

'Well,' he drawled, as he sat back and admired her, 'I guess if a man's to be honest he cain't help but get ideas about a purty-looking gal like you. My friends call me Randy.'

'They do, do they? Hmm . . . ' She raised an eyebrow as she sliced the pie. 'Maybe I'll call you Mac. OK?'

'Do you like custard, Mac?' Rain-in-the-Face asked.

'Sure do, I love it. I got a boy of my own but he ain't as old as you.'

'I might be going to a college, if my family let me.'

'You don't say?'

'Don't raise your hopes too high, Rain. It's up to your father to decide.' She gave a grimace, as she passed around the pie and custard. 'They are not too keen on the idea.'

They chatted some more and Daisy Bradshaw filled him in on the Marquis de Mores and his lady. 'They all but own this town. They imported workers in on the railroad for the meat factory. Mostly immigrants, Italians, Poles and so forth. In fact, we speak twenty different languages in this school. That's why he managed to raise so many men for his posse, some sixty-strong, but I doubt if most could hit a barn door with a .45.'

She suddenly laughed. 'I suppose you could say he imported me, too. I replied to his advertisement.'

McBride asked which way they had

headed, how long they had been gone and frowned when she said they had set out towards Mr Roosevelt's Elk Horn ranch many miles north.

'The Marquis, I understand, said the robbers would have doubled back from the direction they first took. That would have been a hoax.'

'Yeah, maybe it would. But maybe not. They might be hiding out in the Badlands until the chase cools. Did they take any trackers with them?'

'You mean Indians? No, I don't think so.'

'My pa can track,' Rain-in-the-Face said, proudly. 'He can track anything.'

'Wolf Voice is a Cheyenne police officer along at the reservation. He's a fine man. You're not thinking of getting him involved?'

'Maybe. Why not?'

'Because these are dangerous, violent criminals. Why not leave it to the posse?' Daisy asked, crossly. 'Anyway, what I would like to know is just what you plan to do, Mr McBride, if you should happen to catch up with these delinquents?'

'Waal.' He scuffed his chair away and stuck out his long legs. 'That would depend on their response. My object would be to bring them back for trial, but, like you say, these are dangerous men.'

'You mean, if you were forced to and if you could, you would kill them?'

'If they didn't kill me. I'd bring 'em back if I could and then, I guess, they'd be hanged, even the gal. She's the one you say shot the Wells Fargo man.'

'That's what everybody said, but isn't that rather arbitrary justice?'

'That's the way out here in the West, miss. We don't hold with letting lawyers stick their noses in and cause all kinda delays. All they do is talk a lot of hocus pocus about the rights of the criminals and appeal against death sentences saying they had an unhappy childhood, never had a chance and didn't mean to do it. Maybe the young'uns should be given a second chance, but the older ones, no. They got records already and my vote would be hang 'em high.'

'My God! Don't you think they have any rights, that they might be innocent?'

'Nope; in this case no. I believe in the rights of the victims, the family of the Wells Fargo man who got gunned down doing his duty, them who got robbed of their belongings. I believe in the rights of my neighbour, Pop Williams, who was robbed of his herd by these hooligans and faces ruination in his old age. Out here we believe in the law of the Old Testament, not the new.'

'An eye for an eye?'

'That's the way most folks figure it should be. This is a lawless land, Miss Bradshaw, and there's only one way to tame it, with a gun.'

'You've got it all worked out,' she replied, with an expression of contempt, getting to her feet. 'Well, it's been interesting meeting you, McBride.'

He stroked his jaw and stared at her, but appeared to decide it was time he was on his way. 'It's been mighty pleasant and kind of you. Shall I — '

'No. We'll do the dishes. It's getting dark, but I'm sure you'll find yourself a room in town.'

He was tightening Satan's cinch outside under the stars, when she came to the door to say goodnight. 'Huc-come,' he called, 'a good-looker like you ain't wed? This is woman-starved country.'

Daisy smiled, crossed to the fence and hissed, 'I *have* been asked. But to tell the truth I've no wish to become the unpaid cook, scullion, washer-woman and bed-warmer to an uncouth, uneducated male with primitive views on justice. I prefer my independence, even if it is poorly paid.'

'Ouch!' He gave a grin as he got hold of the saddle horn and swung aboard. 'I guess I asked for that.'

'Good hunting, Mr McBride. Or bounty hunting. You heard, I suppose, the Wells Fargo office has issued rewards of five hundred dollars on each of them, alive or dead?'

'No, I didn't know that.' He tugged the powerful black away. 'Not that it makes any difference to me. So long. Maybe we'll meet again. Maybe we won't.'

She watched him go, raised a hand, almost reluctantly, and called, 'Good luck. Take care.'

* * *

Hell Canyon was an arid backwater of the Badlands which only rattlers and coyotes called home. Its high yellowstone cliffs were riddled with small caves in one of which the train robbers had agreed to hole up until the hue and cry died down.

Parrot Nose Johnson figured they were about thirty miles from Medora, but they had taken such a zig-zag course through the maze of ravines he couldn't be sure. In the old days he had marauded out there with Hogan's bunch and had a fair idea of the lie of the land.

'I figure we've thrown 'em off the scent,' he announced that night, as darkness settled on the harsh landscape. He had scanned the area through binoculars and spotted a large cloud of dust being kicked up by what must have been a big posse heading away northwest into the far distance. 'We can sleep easy tonight, boys.'

But the 'boys' were too euphoric about the success of the heist to take much heed. They had tipped their heavily laden saddle-bags out on to a blanket laid out in the cave, and by the light of a sagebrush fire hooted and yelled with amazement as they heaped the greenbacks into one thousand-dollar piles.

'Forty thousand smackeroos!' Joel Doyle cried. 'You ever set your eyes on so much moolah? I'm gonna take my share and head on down to Mexico. Ten thousand dollars will buy me a lifetime's supply of gals and tequila.'

'Hang on a minute.' Johnson tipped his derby over one eye and scratched the back of his head. 'Before you start taking your share nobody said nuthin' about ten thousand.'

The sight of a large amount of cash did strange things to a man and it was having that effect on Joel Doyle. 'What *you* talking about, Johnson?' he demanded in his gruff, surly way. 'Ten thou' for you, ten thou' for me. These other four are jest youngsters and kin have five thousand each. That's fair, ain't it?'

Buzz was down on his knees going through the cash on another blanket tipped from wallets and purses in gold, silver and notes, the rings, stickpins, necklaces, bracelets and assorted jewellery. He looked up and grinned his rotting teeth at them, 'That sounds fair enough to me.'

'Well, it don't to me,' Parrot Nose shouted. 'Who set up this deal? Who runs this outfit? Who's done all the hard-thinking and paid for information? Me, that's who. I told you bozos from the start I was entitled to the lion's share. So, I'm taking twenty thousand.

You others can have the rest 'tween you.'

'Oh, yeah,' Joel growled, 'and jest how do you propose we split?'

'Look at it this way, Doyle; we don't want to fall out over this. You see, boys,' Johnson explained, 'we're like a cattle company. I'm the boss and the Kid, here, is my ramrodder. He's also my explosives expert. You others work for us. You ever heard of cowpokes getting the same share as the boss? Grow up.'

'OK,' Joel said, his muddy eyes malevolent. 'If you're taking twenty, I'm taking twenty. These others can have the cash and jewellery on t'other blanket. Anyhow, who ever heard of equal shares for some damn 'breed, his whore and a coupla snotty-nosed kids.'

There was silence except for the whining of the mountain wind outside as the firelight slopped weird shadows of them on the walls and roof of the cave making them appear to Della like grotesque long-nosed misers crouched counting their hoard.

Parrot Nose Johnson was glad that he had the three-barrel Dickson gripped by its walnut stock in his left hand. 'You still don't understand, do you, Doyle, you half-wit? You're just some no-hoper prairie drifter. You ain't entitled to no major share. Get this in your thick skull for once and for all.' He poked the pile of notes with the shotgun barrel. 'This twenty is mine. This ten goes to the Kid and Della. You lot can have ten thousand 'tween the three of you' — he flicked the bundles towards them — 'is that clear?'

Jim Hetherington, in his shoddy, unwashed garb, looked around, nervously. 'Take it, Joel. You can have it. Me an' Buzz'll take what's on the blanket. That's OK, ain't it, Buzz?'

'Sure,' Buzz agreed, eager to please. 'Looks like a damn fortune to me. It'll do us. We ain't gonna argue.'

'Waal, *I* am.' Joel Doyle flipped the stud that strapped his Colt Navy into its holster and his dirt-engrained hand hovered over the notched butt, his eyes mean and merciless beneath the brim of his hat. 'I'm sick of taking orders from this two-timing, fat-headed scud-belly. Who's he think he is? You with me, boys? Remember, by rights, we oughta have Sam's share.'

The two youngsters glanced at each other anxiously and Jim began tentatively to pull back his goatskin coat, but hesitated. 'We don't want no trouble, Joel.'

'Yes we do!' Doyle hoisted his heavy Colt from the leather holster, but he was no fast shootist, and had it only half-way out when Parrot Nose brought the Dickson up, his left forefinger on the first trigger, guiding the stock with his right palm and fired —

'*Ka-pow!*' The shotgun exploded and Joel Doyle was hurtled onto his back, pellets peppering his chest.

He lay there for moments in shock, a look of disbelief on his face as points of blood spurted out of his shirt. 'Christ Awmighty!' he cried. 'You kilt me, you bastard.'

'Yes, pal,' Parrot Nose replied, as he watched him slump into oblivion. 'You certainly ain't wrong about that.'

The Kid's Allen and Hopkins was in his hand and Della, behind him, had brought out the shiny Smith & Wesson, both business ends aimed at the two scruffy youths.

Buckthorn grinned, tauntingly, as he met their eyes. 'Come on, aincha gonna back your pal? What's wrong, boys?' He began making a clucking sound, 'Chook, chook, chook! You yaller?'

'Leave 'em be,' Johnson ordered, blowing down the first of his three barrels. 'You two dish-swabs can take what's on that blanket. Git outa here now and keep on going. Don't come back. You did your job and earned what's there. It's better than a cow-poke's thirty-a-month, ain't it? Be grateful.'

'We are, Mr Johnson,' Buzz stuttered, down on one knee, tying up the four corners of the blanket and throwing the bundle over his shoulder. 'Mighty grateful, ain't we, Jim? Come on, Jim, let's git outa here.'

'Don't go selling all that jewellery at once,' Johnson said, 'it'll only draw attention to you.'

'We'll head for Colorado,' Jim agreed, easing carefully past them and backing out the cave. 'We'll cash it in piece by piece as and when we need it. You won't see us again.'

'Good sense, boys,' Johnson called, 'Ride hard. You should get through. The posse's miles away.'

When they had gone he beamed at the other two. 'It looks like a clean split, half for you, half for me, don't it, Kid?'

He poked Joel with his boot. 'The nerve of that guy. I never did like his ugly mug. Do me a favour and toss him down the ravine. The wolves and ravens will soon pick him clean.'

9

Although sparsely populated, these three corners of Wyoming, Montana and Dakota were a boiling pot of not only immigrants, settlers, missionaries, drifting cowboys, panhandlers, gunmen, doxies, gamblers, fraudsters, snake-oil salesmen, gold-seekers and tough, land-grabbing cattle barons, but also the haunt of wealthy eccentrics, remittance men and second sons who had been sent out West to try to make their mark.

Perhaps the most eccentric of all was the Marquis de Mores. His French chateau on the Little Missouri had been built of stone, turreted, with its own drawbridge across a specially dug moat, its twenty-six rooms furnished in mock medieval style, no expense spared on its trappings. There was a banqueting hall, billiards room, wine vault, kitchens, and a library stocked with English, German and French books, many of them priceless. The marquis aimed to bring a touch of class and culture to the West. Here, cosseted by a staff of twenty butlers, maids, chefs, footmen, grooms and gardeners, his wife, Medora, reigned as his queen.

While the marquis busied himself with his innumerable and sometimes crackpot business schemes, the marquise would supervise her formal garden, or the clipping of their tennis court, see to the importation of fine wines and delicacies and the daily running of the chateau. Of course, most of the cash came from her own family's banking fortune, and they frittered it liberally. But what else was money for?

Medora de Mores was no indoor girl, however. She loved to ride and go out on hunting expeditions with her husband, travelling in their luxurious hunting coach in which they would spend the nights. Together, the marquis in his uniform, Medora in riding habit, on a fine charger, an eagle feather in her hat, cut quite a colourful dash.

On the night of the robbery she dined alone, if one could be considered alone with twenty servants on call. But she sat at the long banqueting table beneath a brilliant 200-candle chandelier, picking at various courses, entrées, oysters, ortolans, game pie and strawberry ice cream — from their own dairy and ice house — and wondered, as outside the coyotes howled, how long Antoine would be away this time.

★　★　★

Holed up in their eyrie above Hell Canyon, the Buckthorn Kid cradled a Winchester rifle in the crook of his arm and paced back and forth, impatiently, gazing out across the bleak ridges.

'We're wasting time,' he told Johnson the next morning. 'It's time we got out. If they lay seige to us here it would only be a matter of time 'fore we run out of shells but, worst of all, water.'

The only sources of water were the few puddles caught in the rock from the heavy rains of a few days before and that was fast evaporating in the hot sunshine. They were down to using the contents of Joel Doyle's canteen to make coffee.

The Kid looked to Parrot Nose for a reply, but he squatted on a rock, glumly peering through his binoculars at the horizon. He lay them aside, stroked his heavy moustache and muttered, 'I dunno, Kid. If we head out in daylight we're bound to run into 'em. We'd better hang on here and make a break tonight.'

'What's the point of having all this cash,' Della whined, in her sing-song Missouri drawl, 'if we're stuck in these damn breaks and cain't spend it.'

'You're alive, aincha?' Johnson shouted, irritably. 'That's more than Doyle is. Doncha worry, gal, I'll git you out a here.'

★   ★   ★

Meanwhile, the marquis, as always, had a brainwave of a plan and intended to execute it with military precision. He had ridden through the night with his posse, pausing only to leave a bunch of them at every possible line of exit from the Badlands. He would leave one of his trusted ranch-hands or ramrodder in charge, men who could ride and shoot, and show his meat-packers how to handle their guns.

He would ride on again, sometimes leaving a couple of sheepherders to guard a gulch. They were used to roaming these mountains with his herds and knew every coulée. He warned them to keep watch night and day and, if their suspicions were aroused, to shoot first and ask questions later.

By early dawn he had his men strung out in a semi-circle and, arriving at the ranch house of his neighbour, Roosevelt, knocked him up and introduced Wells Fargo officer, Morgan O'Malley, who had exchanged his shredded suit for a new one, and the local representative,

Henry Wells, who ran the office in Medora.

'We need your 'elp, Teddy,' the marquis cried in his heavy French accent. 'If you and your men will join the 'unt we will 'ave these robbers in a noose, as you say, completely bottled up. Then we move in on them, guns blazing.'

'Tally ho, what! The hunt is on. Love to join you, old boy.' Roosevelt ushered them into the Elk Horn dining room for ham and eggs breakfast. 'Calm down, Antoine. Relax. You certainly seem to be in high dudgeon about this.'

'Dudgeon? What is this?'

'I mean mad. In a temper. Better watch your blood pressure.' Roosevelt's eyes twinkled behind his spectacles. 'We've got to tread careful here. Don't want any more chaps getting killed.'

'Mad! Of course I am mad.' The marquis twitched his waxed moustaches fiercely. 'They 'ave stolen ten thousand dollars belonging to me. How dare they? It is a matter of principle.'

'You just drink your coffee, Antoine.

You've had a hard ride. Got to look after the inner man.' Roosevelt pulled on his boots over thick socks and laced them tight, then went to choose a rifle. He returned in a plaid hunting jacket and fur hat. 'I'll go roust up the boys and we'll be ready to ride in ten minutes. Don't you worry, Marquis, we'll catch these cuckoos.'

The two ranchers were unaware that two of the cuckoos, not long out of their nests, had been already caught. Buzz and Jim riding hard along a creek out of the mountains, intent on reaching the wide-open prairie and freedom, ran slap into an ambush arranged by de Mores' ramrodder, Hank Briggs, who, obeying his employer's instructions, had arranged his posse of greenhorns in the shelter of rocks on either side of the creek, and told them to stay alert with weapons primed and ready cocked. Most half-dozed, but towards dawn jumped awake when one shouted, 'Somebody comin'.'

'Yeah, I see'd 'em,' Hank snarled.

'Git ready to fire.'

Buzz was in the lead, charging along the creek on his mustang. Before he knew it explosions were racketing out and bullets whistling about him. He was hit in the head, chest, thigh, and arm, blood gouging from him as his mustang screamed and cartwheeled headlong. They were both dead before they hit the ground.

Jim Hetherington hauled his piebald around, but the terrified horse went up on his back legs, whinnying and flailing his front hoofs as bullets caroomed around them. Hank jumped out of cover and dragged the youth from the saddle as he tried to pull his revolver.

'No you don't,' the ramrodder shouted, slamming his gloved fist into Jim's jaw. 'All right,' he bawled. 'Hold your fire!'

'What we gonna do with him now?' one of his men asked, grabbing hold of the piebald. 'Hey, look at this.' He took the gunny sack of stolen goods from the pommel horn and peered inside. 'Sonuvabitch!'

'I'll take care of this.' Hank rifled through the contents and gave a whistle. 'Quite a haul. You were with them train robbers, were you, boy? You stole this li'l lot? Where's all the cash?'

'We ain't got it.' Jim wiped blood from his mouth as he was hauled to his feet. 'That's our share.'

'You mean it *was*.' Hank gave a brutal laugh.

'Where's the rest of the cash?'

'The others have got it all.'

'Where are they?'

'Back in the hills.'

'Yeah?' Hank put a hand in the gunny sack and poked through the contents, pulling out a wallet stuffed with dollar bills. 'Well, whadda ya know? We're gonna have to return all this to the rightful owners.' He waggled the wallet in the air. 'Minus our li'l reward. Eh, boys?'

He looked at the five men, questioningly. 'There's nigh on a hundred dollars in here. How about twenty dollars each?'

'Sure, why not,' a Polish slaughter-man agreed, with a shrug. 'We deserve something for being out all night.'

The other four men grabbed a fistful of dollars as Hank doled out the cash. Hank pocketed twenty, tossed the wallet away into the rocks and asked, 'What shall we do with him?'

'Shoot the li'l punk,' was the Pole's cold response. 'Don't go begging us for mercy, boy. You didn't show no mercy to that Wells Fargo man.'

'Please, don't do this.' Hetherington could hardly get the words out he was trembling so much. 'It wasn't me. It was them others, Della and the Kid and — '

'You figure you can lead us to them?'

'I don't know, it was dark.'

'You better had know, you yaller li'l runt. Come on, git on your hoss. We'd better take him to the Marquis, boys. He can spill his guts to him. The boss'll want to be in at the kill. Bring the stiffie. There's reward on these boys.'

⋆　⋆　⋆

As for Randy McBride, he had left the Alhambra Hotel in Medora early that morning, collected his stallion and saddle-pack, and set off out of town intent on riding twenty miles east along the rail track to find the scene of the robbery and start his own search. The train and passengers had by now, of course, been moved on to Miles City.

He was, sometime later, almost at the point where the railroad emerged onto the river valley out of the chasm of cliffs when he saw riding towards him a dark and severe-of-mien Indian in a high-bowled hat and gilt-buttoned uniform.

'*Washtay!*' McBride called out his greetings in Siouan and raised a hand. 'Are you the Cheyenne called Wolf Voice?'

'*Wayo!* True. How do you know me?'

'I had supper last night with Miss Bradshaw and your boy, Rain-in-the-Face. I am glad we have met.'

'Why should you be glad of this?' Wolf Voice asked, steadying his mustang. 'Who are you?'

'The name's McBride. Your son told me you are a man who can read spoor. He said you are the best.'

The Cheyenne's face remained impassive. '*Hin?*'

'There's plenty tracks around here. I guess this is where they robbed the train. I want to go after them. Will you help me?'

'I want nothing to do with whiteman's trouble. I police Indian trouble, that is all. I have to go into Medora to see Miss Bradshaw. I will give her my answer about my son. Let me pass.'

McBride pulled the stallion aside and drawled, 'Cain't that wait? One of the robbers was a Sioux.'

'No, he was not one of my people.'

'But it gives you the right to go after him,' the rancher suggested, craftily. 'If you're gonna put your boy through college, it may be a charity, but he's gonna need some cash to see him through. There's bounty of five hundred dollars on each of 'em.'

The Cheyenne stared at him. 'How

did you know I am to say yes to Miss Bradshaw?'

'Because you look like a sensible man. I've got a boy and I wouldn't want to lose his company, but if an offer like this came along I'd say yes, too. I would have to think of what was best for him and his future.'

Wolf Voice nodded and raised his hand. 'We go shares?'

McBride gripped it. 'Down the line, partner. They headed over there into the Badlands. Shall we go?'

'Soon.' The Indian raised his hands to the sun high in the noon sky and cried out, 'Hee-ay-hee-ee!'

McBride guessed he was getting his power from the Great Spirit before he set off on this venture. When he had quit wailing, the Indian sent his horse away at a kind of sideways shuffle, casting about, back and forth. 'Good,' he called, pointing to the ground with a sweep of his hand and set his horse cantering towards the hills.

Parrot Nose Johnson had been sat on his rock for a long time in thinker attitude, his fist to his brow. 'I've got it,' he shouted, jumping to his feet.

'Got what?' Della asked.

'The way out of here. We're going back to Medora.'

'You're crazy,' the Kid protested. 'What we wanna do that for?'

'Didn't you see it when you were there?'

'See what?'

'No, you were too busy addling your brains in some alehouse. But I took a look around town and that marquis whatever they call him has got a luxury Pullman coach and locomotive on a siding in the rail yards. He uses the line as his own private railroad.'

'So what?' the Kid asked, impatiently.

'So, Della, you're going down there and find an engineer and, at the point of your gun, get him to fire the thing up. It takes an hour or two to get the puffer ready to roll.'

'You are crazy,' she protested. 'I can't just ride in there.'

'Why not,' Johnson growled. 'The town'll be deserted. They're all out looking for us. I seen their dust. You go in there, gal, and make sure that thang is ready to go. We're riding out of here in style.'

'Hot damn!' The Kid gave a whoop of glee, slapping his thigh. 'Mr Johnson you're a genius. Where we gonna go.'

'We'll head west along the railroad seventy miles to Glendive or maybe Stanley's Stockade, then cross the Yellowstone and disappear up along the Musselshell. They'll never catch us.'

'So, while I'm hijacking a locomotive,' Della put in, 'what will you and the Kid be up to?'

'Us?' Parrot Nose Johnson gave her a beaming smile and went to saddle his horse. 'We're gonna go and git us our passport *out*. Nobody'll dare touch us. We'll — '

As he spoke a slug suddenly whined

past his head, ricocheting away, the crack of a rifle followed by its echo bouncing off the cliff wall.

Parrot Nose ducked down, dragging his mustang into cover. 'Hot dang,' he cried. 'There's somebody down there.'

'Two somebodies,' the Kid replied as another report, a puff of smoke and the crooning wail of a bullet made him, too, jump back. 'Who the hell are they?'

'Kill them,' Johnson roared, pouring a fusillade of revolver fire down into the canyon. As the Kid and Della joined in the attack it was the turn of a tall man in a dusty, dark jacket and an Indian in police uniform to dodge out of the way and find concealment in the rocks.

For half an hour there was a lively exchange of leaden compliments but eventually it slowed into a stalemate.

'What the hell they doing down there?' the Kid asked, peering down his rifle sights.

McBride and Wolf Voice were having a pow wow. 'There's no way we're gonna dislodge 'em like this. We're just wasting lead,' the rancher said, pumping out empty shells from his smoking carbine.

Wolf Voice studied the curiously shaped cliff. There was an overhang above the outlaws. 'Maybe I go round the back and get up above them, flush 'em out?'

McBride squinted up and growled, 'I dunno.'

'You wait here 'til I give signal, OK?' The Cheyenne didn't wait for McBride to agree, but dodged away along the foot of the cliff through the rubble of big rocks.

'Maybe it's the only way,' McBride muttered.

Sweat trickled down his temple as the late afternoon sun blazed down. 'No wonder they call this Hell Creek,' he muttered. He had loose-hitched Satan to a sage bush back down the creek with the mustang and heard him whinnying shrilly. Vaguely, he wondered what was worrying him. The Indian seemed to have been gone an age.

Suddenly he saw him appear, creeping over the top of the loaf-shaped crag above the outlaws. As suddenly, they made their move, before Wolf Voice could get his sights on them, riding out from the cave and charging in line down the scree of the hill, one behind the other, leaping their mounts over rocks, plunging into dust and ploughing on down towards McBride as if uncaring that they might break their necks or a horse's leg in the descent.

Taken by surprise, McBride managed to snap off a couple of shots from his Spencer, levering slugs into the breech, aiming at the leading rider, a ruddy-faced older man. But their wild, zig-zag motion made him miss, and although he stood his ground until the last moment, when three crack shootists came charging at him, hand-guns blazing, he was forced to scramble back out of the way to save his own life.

'Hot damn!' he yelled, lying on his back in the dust watching them go.

But, even worse, as Satan heard the

explosions, saw the riders charging towards him, he screamed with frantic terror and by sheer brute force dragged the sage bush from its precarious hold on the rock and fled.

Wolf Voice, crouched on top of the rock, was equally dismayed. He had been unable to get an accurate shot in and his own mustang, breaking free, had been fazed by the robbers and set off after the stallion with herd instinct, kicking and high-tailing away at top speed.

There was nothing to do but climb back down to McBride who scowled at him. 'We've lost 'em now. That damn stallion of mine could keep on running for twenty miles. It's my fault. I didn't know he was gunshy. He ain't never been tested like that before.'

Wolf Voice slapped his shoulder. 'Come on. The horses are tired. They have already done forty miles. They won't go far.'

'Far enough. By the time we catch 'em those three will be miles away.'

'I watch them from top of cliff. It look like they go back towards Medora.'

'Medora? What would they do that for? Hey, maybe you're right. The marquis's plan has a flaw. He thought he could bottle 'em up, but he's left his bottle uncorked at the neck.'

'Come,' Wolf Voice grunted, shouldering his carbine. 'We go.'

★   ★   ★

'It is going to be in your interests at your trial you help us,' the Marquis de Mores warned Jim Hetherington. 'You must lead us to where they are.'

'Ol' Four Eyes', as Roosevelt was affectionately known to his men, had led his cowboys out on the round-up to try to seal off the eastern side of this section of the Badlands, while the marquis had returned to be met by Hank and his captive.

'All I remember is it looked like some kinda cottage loaf,' the luckless Jim whined, as he led the uniformed marquis and his men back towards Hell Creek. 'Yuh, thar 'tis, yuh honour,' he cried later, pointing upwards, trying to ingratiate himself.

Antoine de Mores fired a shot up at the cliff, but there was no response. When he sent a couple of men up to take a look eventually, one yelled back down, 'They been here. But they've gawn.'

The marquis hacked viciously at his horse with frustration, whirling it around. 'Let us see if we can find their tracks.'

'What'll we do with him?' Hank took a bite at a plug of baccy and chewed slowly, nodding at the youth.

The marquis pointed his riding crop at a lone pine that had managed to make purchase on the rocks, a spur of a branch jutting out over them.

'Hang him,' he snapped, before riding away down the creek.

10

'Look at this joint!' Parrot Nose Johnson exclaimed as he and Buckthorn cantered their mustangs along the bank of the Little Missouri River and spotted the turreted French chateau set back amid its garden. 'Who does that mark-ee think he *is*?'

'He's left his door open to welcome us,' the Kid replied, seeing that the medieval drawbridge was down, but he was beginning to have doubts about this operation. 'Hell, Mr Johnson, why don't we just git on the dang train an' go? This is askin' for trouble.'

'Faint heart ne'er won fair lady.' Johnson gave a caustic laugh and cantered on across the bridge into the courtyard. It was deserted so he jumped down and hammered the knocker of a big oak door. It creaked open and an elderly flunkey in a penguin suit poked his nose out. 'Yes, sir, can I help you?'

'Sure can,' Johnson growled. 'We got a message from the mark-ee for his missus. We got to give it to her personally.' He pushed into the house and said, 'Just show us the way.'

It was 7.00 p.m. by the clock and the raven-haired Medora was in her bedroom being buttoned into her taffeta evening dress by her maid in readiness to dine. A lady always dressed for dinner and it was a habit Medora never neglected even when she was alone. There were certain standards an aristocrat, or even a banker's daughter, had to uphold.

Before she could reply to a tap on the door her flustered major domo was ushered in. 'Madam,' he began, 'two gentleman — '

A man in a brown derby, his ruddy face reflected by his even more redolent check suit, over which was draped a stained duster coat, thrust the butler aside and pointed a three-barrel shotgun at her, his beady brown eyes malicious. 'Howdy, lady. You're coming with us.'

'What?' The raven-haired Medora eyed him, haughtily. 'Are you mad? Get out of here. How dare you?'

When Parrot Nose reached out to grab hold of her wrist she fell back on the four-poster bed and screamed, shrilly. As the butler tried to intervene, Johnson cracked him across the jaw with the barrel of the shotgun and he collapsed on the floor. The maid joined in and tried to grapple with him for the shotgun.

'OK, I got her,' the Kid shouted, hooking an arm around the woman's neck and hurling her back to tumble on top of the major domo. 'You two, just quit it, if you wanna stay in one piece.' He pointed a black-gloved finger at them. 'We're taking this dame hostage. We ain't gonna hurt her.'

Medora had other ideas, however, taking advantage of the distraction to roll lithely across the four-poster bed and scramble to open a bedside drawer.

She pulled out her silver-enscrolled revolver, gritted her teeth and fired at the beaky-nosed intruder. The shot cut a streak of blood across Johnson's right temple.

Furious, he was about to blast her to extinction when the Kid leapt across, pushing the shotgun aside, and landed on top of her. He got hold of her wrist, back-handing her across the cheek, and twisted the revolver from her hand, tossing it away.

Medora kicked, struggled and screamed as the Kid shouted, 'Calm down, you wild cat.' When she did so and lay staring angrily into his dark eyes, he smiled perfect white teeth as he felt her body's perfumed warmth beneath him and glanced down at her milk-white bosom rising and falling, seductively. 'No need to get agitated.'

'Right,' Johnson bellowed, sweeping his Dickson in an arc to cover them. 'We're taking her out of here. We don't want no more trouble. Come on, Kid, what you playing at?'

'Ah,' Buckthorn groaned, feeling movement amid his black leathers, 'she's some woman, ain't she?' He caught her by the chin with his right hand, and with his left ran his fingers down the rustling turquoise taffeta dress, jerking it up over her stockinged legs. 'Cain't you give me ten minutes to teach this stuck-up hussy a thing or two?'

'We ain't got time for that. Get on your damn feet, you sex-crazy Sioux. Bring her with you and make sure she don't try any more tricks. Here' — he pulled free a cord from the bed curtains — 'tie her wrists. Better do 'em in front so she can hang on to her hoss.'

'Where are you taking me?' Medora demanded, tossing back her hair as she was manhandled to her feet. 'My husband will hunt you down and kill you both for this.'

'Don't you worry,' Buckthorn grinned, dragging her out of the room and down the stairs after Johnson. 'You and me are gonna have plenty of time to be together soon as we git on the train. We're going on a long journey.' He circled an arm around her slim waist and gave her breast a squeeze. 'I'll git rid of Della. She can guard the damn driver up front. We'll be alone.'

'Don't touch me, you trash,' Medora moaned. 'I'll have you flogged — '

'Shut it, sister,' Johnson shouted, stepping out of the front door. 'Where's your bronc? Let's get it saddled.'

They found her white mare in the stables and a boy groom, under threat, quickly had it saddled. Johnson snatched a rawhide lariat from the pommel and tossed the noose over Medora's head, jerking it tight around the throat. 'Climb aboard, lady,' he ordered, as he got on the back of his mustang, sticking the shotgun in the saddle holster and paying out the rope, 'and don't forget, you try anything and I'll drag you along by your damn neck.'

'You better do what he says,' the Kid told her, as he vaulted on to his own bronc. 'He's real mean. He'd jest as soon kill you as spit.'

Medora sat astride, her dress hitched up, hanging on to the saddle horn with her bound hands. She scowled malevolently at them and made no reply. However, she deemed it wise to knee the mare forward as they moved away and the lariat tautened. 'Come on, Bess,' she whispered. 'Keep up for God's sake.'

After that, as they rode wildly back towards Medora, all she could do was pray that the half-breed did not have his way or the Parrot-beaked man shot-gun her. 'God help me,' she moaned.

★ ★ ★

It took an hour before McBride and Wolf Voice caught up with their horses. They found them grazing peacefully on a patch of grass beside a trickling stream.

'Come on,' the rancher said, mounting up, 'we got a good two-hour ride back to Medora.'

The rest seemed to have refreshed the animals, although the stallion was all heart and could gallop for miles. The wiry, brindled mustang, like his breed could, too, survive on barely any sustenance and carry its rider on. They had already travelled forty or so miles that day and had another twenty to go, but the horses faced the task with fortitude and ate up the distance at a steady lope.

* * *

Della had found it easier than she had believed possible to ride into town, find a greasy-overalled engineer loitering in the marquis's engine sheds and persuade him to fire up The Flyer, as it was called. An occasional prod behind his ear with her new S & W kept him busy, but it was a nerve-racking business waiting for the Kid and Johnson to arrive.

'We're ready to go,' the engineer announced, proudly, wiping his oily hands and pressing a lever to hiss out steam. 'But you're gonna have to help stoke the engine with logs from the tender.'

'Aw, I may be a gal but I ain't afeared of hard work. I been raised tough. The line to Glendive is clear, ain't it?'

'Yep, nuthin' due through 'til Thursday.'

'In that case you better link up with the Pullman and get it out on the main line.'

'Do you want me to drop off these empty goods vans first? That's gonna take time and I need someone who knows what he's doing to help out.'

'No, just stick the Pullman on the back. Show me what to do and I'll jine her up when you give the sign.'

'You know, gal,' the engineer said, as she jumped back in the cab the operation completed, 'you'd make a good railroadman. You ever think of going straight I'd give you a job an' maybe we could git hitched, too.'

'Thanks for the offer, granpa, but I'm

spoken for and from here on it's the high life for me. We're headin' fer Cal-ee-for-nay-ay! Where the hell them two gotten to?'

As she spoke, Johnson and the Kid came charging into Medora closely followed by a girl on a white mare, her skirts blown up by the breeze showing the whites of her thighs between her stocking tops and her rucked-up drawers. 'Who the hell's she?' Della wailed.

'She's her ladyship, Mrs Mark-ee.' Buckthorn pulled in his bronc alongside the steaming locomotive cab. 'Howdy, mister, you ready to blow? Remember, we want top speed all the way to Stanley's Stockade' — he spun his revolver on his finger — 'or else! You keep him covered, Della, we'll put this wild-cat in the coach.' He gave a whoop of delight. 'See you at t'other end, gal. Let's go.'

The Flyer began to huff out spirals of smoke as its brakes were released, the couplings jerked and clanged, and it slowly moved away.

Buckthorn jumped from his mustang, unbuckling the saddle-bags stuffed with a fortune in greenbacks, ordered Medora down at gunpoint, and a jab in the back with the Allen and Hopkins urged her to step up before him onto the Pullman as it slowly approached. Parrot Nose kept his Dickson at the ready, glancing around at the deserted town. It was 9.00 p.m. and almost dark. His own saddle-bags on his shoulder, he hauled himself up onto the rear viewing platform as they rattled away.

'Hot damn,' the Kid hooted, his boots up on a divan in the Pullman's luxuriously appointed drawing-room. 'We've done it!'

'Yeah!' Parrot Nose's face lit up a beaming smile. 'Ye of little faith. I told you we would. You gotta trust me, Kid. Hey, look at this bar stocked with booze. Fancy some champagne, your ladyship?'

'Shall I untie her now?'

'Why not?' Johnson popped the cork

on the bottle and filled glasses as the train gathered speed. Clouds of smoke drifted past the windows, and they heard its engine reverberating, the rods rattling rythymically, as they clacked along the rail. Its bell clanged mournfully. 'We're on our way. Might as well make ourselves comfortable. We got a long ride. Yes, we've done it, Kid. Here's to us.'

Medora eased her sore wrists as the rope was released, straightened her dress, tried, with woman's vanity, to rearrange her wind-straggled hair. 'Yes,' she mused, 'I might as well. I'm dying of thirst. My husband did pay for it after all.'

She accepted a glass of bubbly and sat in a padded armchair sipping at it modestly, staring at them with her vivid violet eyes. 'Well, I certainly didn't expect this.'

'It sure is some lifestyle,' the Kid remarked, gazing at her. 'That Froggy's a lucky guy to have all this an' a bobbydazzler like you as his plaything.'

'You know,' Johnson beamed, topping up their glasses, 'I thought I was past it, but this gorgeous gal is even giving an old man like me funny ideas. There's a bed in the adjoining compartment, Kid, why don't you enjoy yourself?' He gave a broad wink. 'I might even take a second turn.'

'No!' Medora began to kick and scream again as Buckthorn caught hold of her around the waist, only pausing to pick up his saddle-bags filled with dollars, and hoisted her bodily through the door into the bedroom. 'You can't be serious? Let me go, you stinking no-good.'

Johnson chuckled and tipped the bottle to his lips. He suddenly froze as he caught sight through the window of two riders, one on a black stallion, one on a mustang, galloping their horses along the side of the track beside the coach. He panicked and looked around for his shotgun. Was it loaded? He pulled the awkward side-opening stock to one side to check it was and clacked it back. 'Kid!' He yelled.

But the Kid had his hands full, the woman beneath him on the bed as they were rattling and jogging on their way . . .

McBride and Wolf Voice had arrived at Medora to see the private train steaming away, smoke pouring from its stack towards the west. 'What the hell's happening?' he asked. 'Come on, we gotta catch that coach.'

Together, the two riders went pounding in an arc across the plain, slowly catching up with the locomotive which had reached a speed of thirty miles an hour. 'C'mon, Satan,' McBride yelled, hanging over the stallion's neck and whacking him either side with his wrist quirt. 'You can do it.'

Slowly, gradually, they caught up, galloping on either side of the Pullman coach. Suddenly, a window was smashed and the snout of a treble-barrel poked through. Before Wolf Voice could draw back there was an explosion, shot blasted out and he and his mustang went tumbling into the dust and rubble, parting company.

Parrot Nose ran to the other window, smashed that, poked out the shotgun and took another shot, but McBride had his revolver out and fired across from his galloping horse. The bullet creased Johnson's knuckles with searing pain, making him drop the Dickson, which went tumbling away.

'Kid!' He yelled again, grimacing and backing away towards the bedroom door. 'I need your help here.'

McBride made a leap from his saddle to clutch the rails of the back platform. For moments he was suspended, kicking and writhing, then twisted over and onto the platform. Without hesitation he kicked open the door and went in, fanning the hammer of the Remington.

Parrot Nose Johnson hauled out his revolver and fired simultaneously, but a sudden jolt of the train ruined his aim, and he gasped and went kicking backwards through the bedroom door, three slugs in his chest.

The Kid had been having problems

of his own, Medora having groped for the bottle by the bedside and landed him a hefty whack across his cranium. He staggered to his feet as Johnson came back-pedalling through, caught hold of him in his arms as a shield, had his Hopkins out like greased lightning and snapped off two quick shots at McBride.

Medora screamed as the Kid dropped Johnson's bleeding body, snatched up his saddle-bags and, still firing, backed away through the far door of the Pullman. He slammed it shut and climbed to the roof of a rattling and rolling goods van, running along it and leaping for the second one. He turned and lay flat, quickly reloading, waiting for McBride to appear.

The rancher had dodged to one side to avoid the 'breed's fire. When he was gone he prowled forward into the stateroom boudoir and saw a dark-haired woman on the bed, her dress disarranged and screaming, hysterically.

'OK, I'm on your side,' he shouted,

and stepped over Johnson's recumbent body. He let himself out of the Pullman carefully and eased himself up to peer over the top of the goods van. The two vans before him in the darkness, amid the swirling smoke, appeared to be clear of danger. But he wasn't careful enough. As he hauled himself up a slug smashed into his shoulder with the impact of a sledge hammer, knocking him back. McBride hung on desperately with his good arm as the wheels and track flashed by beneath him, fighting the nausea in him, the pain, and attempting to right himself.

Meanwhile, the Kid had got to his feet and run further forwards. He saw Della climbing over the piled high logs of the tender towards him. She clambered up onto the roof of the goods van. 'What's going on?' she shouted.

'Get down,' the Kid yelled, but their words were drowned by the noise of the engine and the wind. The saddle-bags over his shoulder, he stood and watched for his assailant as Della came to hang on beside him on the roof of the rattling iron van. 'I think I got him, whoever he was.'

But, no, with a superhuman effort McBride had pulled himself up to the roof of the van beyond them, his Remington spurting flame as the Flyer howled out a warning with its steam whistle, 'Whooo-ah-ooh!'

McBride tottered on along the roof, holding his wounded shoulder, as the half-Sioux returned fire, bullets carooming past the rancher's head. Suddenly he saw they were entering a tunnel blasted through a side of a hill and threw himself flat. He stared with horror at the Kid and Della as they stood there, unaware. They would be decapitated. There was a great billow of smoke as they entered the black hole and disappeared.

The black tunnel seemed to go on endlessly, McBride choking from grit and smoke, until they came out under the stars again. There was no sign of Della or the Kid. He crawled forward, climbed across to the front coach, and signalled to the engine driver, who, luckily, was looking back, and finally began to apply his brakes.

The train came to a halt with a screeching jolt. Medora pulled herself together and clambered down to the track. She found the engineer tending to McBride as he lay on the logs of the tender. 'We better leave him here,' he shouted down to her. 'He's losing blood fast. I'll make full speed back to Medora. That OK, Miss?'

'Yes, for God's sake, hurry.' She climbed up onto the tender as the driver returned to his cab and put The Flyer into reverse motion. She removed the rancher's bandanna and used it as a pad, holding it tight to try to staunch the flow from the wound. 'You're going to be OK,' she insisted. 'Just hold on.'

McBride looked up at her. 'What about them other two? We better take a look for their bodies.'

'Oh, there'll be plenty of time tomorrow for that. I want to thank you.'

She regarded him, anxiously. 'You won't say anything to my husband about what happened back there?'

'What 'n hell do you think I am?' he muttered before drifting into unconsciousness.

11

The Marquis de Mores had summoned most of his posse by prearranged gunfire signal and, at their head, galloped back at full tilt to Medora. There a breathless, tearful maidservant gasped out that his wife, Medora, had been kidnapped.

'What?' he screamed. 'This is an outrage.' When an old-timer pointed out that they had taken his train and gone west he nearly had apoplexy, his face taking on a crimson hue.

Teddy Roosevelt had heard the gunshots and led his men around from the east, cutting through the hills to investigate. Even though darkness was closing in and they had already covered forty miles, he urged the ranch hands to follow him on into town to see what was going on. Sixty miles in the saddle was nothing to 'Ol' Four Eyes' who, in future days as president of the USA would give his aides palpitations by his jaunts off on horseback for days at a time, through raging blizzards, returning hale and hearty to the White House.

But right now, he found the agitated marquis addressing his men by the light of tar flares at the railroad station. 'I will not rest until my wife is safe,' he shrieked at them, hardly able to keep his monocle in place. 'I offer a five thousand-dollar reward to the man who saves her life. To horse!'

Both parties then went galloping off along the railroad track but they hadn't gone more than two miles when they suddenly saw The Flyer coming charging back through the night, its siren wailing, towards them. They hurriedly cleared the line and chased back after it.

The next thing Randolph McBride knew he was being handed down from the tender into the arms of a crowd of concerned men, as the marquis stepped forward, embraced him and gave him a kiss to both cheeks. '*Merci, m'sieu*,' the Frenchman sobbed. 'Thank you.'

'Ouch!' McBride exclaimed, trying to extricate himself, as the wound in his shoulder began to bleed again. 'This hurts like hell, but it weren't nuthin', pal.'

'We want to offer you the hospitality of our house and best medical treatment while you recuperate.' The dark-haired Medora was smiling radiantly again, hanging onto her husband's arm. 'Nothing would be too much for us.'

Roosevelt grinned and patted the marquis's shoulder. 'All's well that ends well. I trust you won't forget that five thousand dollar reward!'

'What you all hangin' round here for?' McBride growled. 'You better go look for my partner, Wolf Voice. I'm worried about him.'

At that moment, however, who should come riding through the crowd but the Cheyenne policeman himself, on the back of Satan. 'I lost my own hoss,' he explained, 'but I found yours.'

'Good fellow.' McBride suddenly felt

his knees buckling and he hung onto his shoulder to support himself just as Miss Daisy Bradshaw and Rain-in-the-Face pushed through the throng to them.

'How are you?' she asked, gripping his hand in hers. 'We . . . I have been so worried.'

'I'd be fine enough if somebody'd git this dang slug outa my shoulder and quit all this nattering.'

'Would you like to come back with me?' she asked, hesitantly. 'I would look after you.'

A sudden smile lit up McBride's face. 'That sounds like an offer I cain't refuse.' He put his other arm around her shoulder and supported by Daisy and Wolf Voice walked away unsteadily. 'No need to worry about me, Medora,' he called back. 'I'm in good hands now.'

★   ★   ★

As the tunnel loomed up Della had glanced back and saw it in the nick of time. As a great cloud of black smoke

211

engulfed them she had grabbed hold of the Buckthorn Kid and, intentionally or not, they had both toppled off the goods van as it disappeared into the hole and had gone tumbling and cartwheeling down a gravelly slope until they came to rest in a pile of rocks at the bottom of the hill.

'Hell's bells,' the Kid had groaned as he picked himself up and brushed himself down. First he made sure he still had the cash-stuffed saddle-bags with him, then looked around for the girl. 'You OK, Della?'

'Whoo! I think so.' She straightened her floppy hat that had fallen over her nose. 'Don't seem to have no broken bones. Lost my S & W, thassall.'

'Yeah, well, I've lost my new hat and I cain't see nuthin' 'til the moon comes up,' the Kid replied, stumbling around. 'You know somethang, gal? We're lucky to be alive.'

'You're not kiddin', Kid.'

'Come on. Git on your feet. We gotta git outa here.'

'Can't we wait 'til morning?'

'Don't be a damn fool. They'll be out lookin' for us by then. And don't suggest we follow the railroad 'cause that's the first place they'll look. We gotta git right away from here. We'll head west across the prairie.'

'But there ain't nuthin' out there fer miles an' miles an' miles. How can we cross it without hosses?'

'We'll walk. That's what we'll do. Travel by night, hide up by day. Get a move on, you dopey doxy. We gotta be right away from here by dawn. You better keep up or I'm leavin' ya.'

Della, in her rubber topcoat, straggled after him, calling out plaintively through the darkness, 'Hang on, Kid, wait for me.'

'Just move your ass,' he shouted. 'What did I tell ya?'

'Gawd,' she cried, as she caught up. 'I know you say you're called the Buckthorn Kid 'cause you're Buck Thorn's kid, but in my opinion its 'cause you're such a prickly sonfuvabitch.'

By morning, guided by the stars, they were far out on the desolate plain. 'We'll go a few more miles,' the Kid said, 'but be ready to dive for cover.'

He took off his new high-heeled boots and slung them around his neck because he figured he could walk freer without them. When she asked how they would survive without supplies, he replied, 'I know how, Della. I'm a Sioux.'

When he finally allowed her to rest on a grassy knoll he offered her the raw meat of a tortoise that he had killed with his knife. 'You gotta try an' eat it, Della,' he advised, 'if we're gonna get to California.'

'California, is that where we're going?' She lay back and smiled up at him toothily. 'You sure you want me along?'

'Sure I do.' He lay back beside her. 'There or Oregon. They say it's good country out there. We'll be able to buy our own ranch, maybe even raise a family, who knows? With this kinda cash we can do anythang.'

'Will we see the ocean?' she asked. 'They say its bigger'n a lake and never-ending. I allus wanted to see the ocean.'

'We sure will, gal. Now we better git some sleep.'

Della nestled into him and whispered, 'You know, Kid, I didn't mean to kill that Wells Fargo guard. I just saw red. He suddenly seemed like one of them men who'd been stopping me gettin' what I wanted all my life. All them men who've used me, abused me. Them cruel, horrible ones.'

'Yeah, well, he weren't one of them. But you gotta live with it, Della. You killed him. It was one of those thangs that happen. We was robbin' that train and he was tryin' to stop us. What more could you do, gal?'

'No, but, well, it ain't that I'm scared of dying, or hanging. They got a right to do that if they catch me. It's just that I feel kinda sick of that life. All them men. I wanna go straight, I wanna feel clean, Buckthorn.'

'Sure, why not?' He turned and gave her a kiss on the cheek. 'We can be honest. It'll be boring. No more blowin' up trains. But why not? Now *can* I git my rest?'

After all the excitement, the hard-riding, hard-fighting and hard-walking they slept deeply through the day in a nest in the grass and, as the sun began to set in streamers of crimson and gold, got up and walked on together into the West.

'Come on, Della,' the Kid called, taking her hand. 'We ain't gonna hit the Bozeman Trail 'less you go a bit faster.'

'Aw, you,' the girl replied, 'you're allus nagging.'

* * *

When the town medic had taken the bullet out of McBride's shoulder, dosing him with whiskey and getting Daisy to hold him down as he gritted his teeth at the pain, their patient went

216

into a deep coma.

The rancher drifted in and out of consciousness for how many days he did not know. Sometimes he would awake in the afternoon in the brass bed in the upstairs room and see her sitting nearby, silent and composed, gently sewing. Or she would be gone and all he could hear was the distant chanting of school-children. Or were they angels?

Sometimes in the dark night he would break out of some nightmare, sweat pouring from him, and cry out for Rose until he remembered that she was gone, and maybe he was going to join her, too. But Miss Bradshaw would come with a lantern and wipe his brow, and look at his bloody bandage, her touch like that of another ministering angel.

But one day he woke and the sun was shining and he saw her standing smiling at him, a tray in her hands. 'Do you think you're able to sit up today and try some broth?' she asked.

She helped him struggle up, arranging the pillows behind him. 'You've had a bad fever, but I think the worst of it's broken. You've been sweating something terrible. I think it's time I gave you a bed bath.'

'Hey,' he growled, when she tried later. 'I kin bath myself.'

'Well, I never thought you'd be shy, McBride. Come on, don't be bashful. I'm fully conversant with male physiology. I did have brothers.'

Some days later he had managed to get out back to the privy by himself, but was still feeling weak as a kitten from loss of blood. 'I'll be on my way soon,' he said, as he sank back into bed. 'I won't have to bother you.'

'It's no bother.' She sat on the edge of the bed and studied him intently. 'I like having you here.'

McBride met her green eyes and grinned. 'Ya know,' he said, 'I must be my old self. You make me feel horny' — he reached out to grasp her shoulders and pull her towards him, planting a hard kiss on her lips — 'why doncha roll into bed with me?'

Daisy pushed him away, her eyes sparkling. 'Randy by name and randy by nature, eh? Is that all you want of me.'

'Nope,' he drawled, 'I wancha to be my wife.'

'Really? In that case, it's different.' Her lips were soft and responsive as she leaned forwards to kiss him. 'But you'll have to wait to the end of summer term.'

When the children had broken up for the holiday, Daisy gave in notice to the marquis and, along with Rain-in-the-Face and Wolf Voice they travelled on the railroad to Miles City. There, summoned by telegraph, waiting for him on their buggy were Ramon, Marie, Matt, and Pop Williams, and glad they were to see the newlyweds.

McBride hugged his son and drawled, 'Meet your new ma, an' this here's my godson, Rain-in-the-Face. He'll be staying with us 'til September then Daisy's taking him to college in St Louis.'

'Gee, can I go there, too, one day, Dad?'

'Maybe.' McBride turned to Wolf Voice. 'We'll look after your boy, don't worry.' He took a packet from his pocket. 'This here's your share of the reward, partner. The railroad gave us a percentage of the twenty thousand recovered from Parrot Nose and what with five thousand from the marquis we ain't done so bad.'

He turned to Pop and handed him another packet. 'You take this, old-timer. Get on your feet again and the ranch restocked. No, don't refuse. It ain't exactly the cash they stole from you, but it's what they earned me by their misdeeds. So, I say it's yours.'

The rancher swung Daisy around by her waist. 'Now, 'fore we go home, we're all gonna sample the delights of Miles City. I could eat me a horse, which reminds me, I better go get Satan out of his box.'

'Pa, can me an' Rain go see the new roller-skatin' rink?'

'Sure, go on,' he called, 'we'll jine ya.'

When they had run off he gave the

smiling Daisy a hug and a kiss. 'I figure we're all gonna git along jest fine. I might even build a new schoolhouse out at Pumpkin Creek. There could well be a few more kids need teaching their letters out that way soon.'

'They ain't found them two who got away with the missing twenty thousand dollars,' Pop exclaimed. 'But I guess as soon as they start spending them new notes a bounty hunter'll be after 'em.'

'Yeah,' McBride mused, 'maybe I'll go out and take a look for 'em, myself.'

'Come on,' Daisy said, taking his arm. 'Let 'em go. You've done your bit. Or I'll put a ball and chain on you.'.

Afterword

The characters and events in this story are fictional with the exception of Theodore Roosevelt and the Marquis de Mores.

When, as president, Roosevelt invaded Spain's Philippines, he remembered the stoical Westerners he had lived among and recruited many into an armed cavalry, his Rough Riders.

The marquis returned to France after his grandiose ventures crumbled, became involved in the Dreyfus scandal, and was, soon after, murdered by highway robbers while travelling in North Africa.

We do hope that you have enjoyed reading this large print book.

Did you know that all of our titles are available for purchase?

We publish a wide range of high quality large print books including:
Romances, Mysteries, Classics
General Fiction
Non Fiction and Westerns

Special interest titles available in large print are:
The Little Oxford Dictionary
Music Book, Song Book
Hymn Book, Service Book

Also available from us courtesy of Oxford University Press:
Young Readers' Dictionary
(large print edition)
Young Readers' Thesaurus
(large print edition)

For further information or a free brochure, please contact us at:
Ulverscroft Large Print Books Ltd.,
The Green, Bradgate Road, Anstey,
Leicester, LE7 7FU, England.
Tel: (00 44) **0116 236 4325**
Fax: (00 44) **0116 234 0205**

BUZZARD'S BREED

David Bingley

When Jim Storme went to join his brother Red, and his cousin, Bart McGivern, in Wyoming, he was heading for trouble. Cattle barons were attacking lesser men, and branding them as rustlers . . . Jim joined the cattlemen's mercenaries, but he changed sides when confronted by his brother, Red. When a wagon loaded with dynamite hit their ranch, it was one of many clashes between settlers and invaders in which the three Texans made their mark, and struggled to survive.

'LUCKY' MONTANA

Clayton Nash

Sean Rafferty wanted money to buy back the ruins of his family's estate in Ireland. He didn't care how he got that money or how many lives he ruined in the process . . . A man called 'Lucky' Montana found that fate threw him into the deal. With a bounty hunter already stalking him, Montana now had to contend with Rafferty's murderous crew as well . . . Now he must stride into battle, knowing that there is always a bullet waiting for him.